The Gulf Between Us

The Westshore Beach Series

Book One

JULIET BRANDYWINE

For Steve, Rachel, Matthew, and Mom.

PROLOGUE

Eight Years Ago

The day of Emily and Jason's wedding, Cancún, Mexico

Emily glanced between her mom and her best friend, confused.

"I don't understand," she said.

"Jason wasn't on the plane," Jess repeated, more slowly this time.

"But *why* wasn't he on the plane?"

"No one knows for sure."

Jess stood awkwardly along the wall of the resort bungalow, more serious than Emily had ever seen her. Next to Jess, her mom worried her lip, folded her arms as if she were cold, and spared a quick glance for her best friend.

In the distance, a seabird announced its presence with a sharp cry.

"If you guys are trying to play a trick on me, it isn't funny." Emily met her mom's eyes. "Is this some sort of joke?"

"It's not a joke, Em," her mom said gently.

Ignoring their stares—which ranged from pity to shock—Emily picked up her cell and dialed Jace's number again. She'd had trouble with the service all week, and had only spoken to her fiancé once, a few days ago.

She tried to think. Had that been Tuesday? Wednesday?

"Maybe he caught a different flight." Emily looked up when the phone connected directly to Jace's voicemail without ringing. "He's not answering, but that could mean anything. He could be on the plane right now and have his cell turned off. And I don't have a great signal here."

Another look passed between Jess and her mom.

Emily swallowed and forced herself to take a deep breath. "Something's happened to him then. You can tell me. What's happened? Where's Jace?"

"Ty just got back from the airport." Jess played with the tassel on her purse, avoiding Emily's eye. "The gate agent was…open to influence."

"Tyler bribed the gate agent?"

"You know Ty," Jess said with a momentary wry smile. "He could charm the fur off a mink."

"And?"

Her mom glanced away, busying herself with adjusting her sky-blue dress.

"No one by the name of Jason Williams is listed on any flight arriving from Tampa yesterday, today, or tomorrow," Jess said.

"But that doesn't make any sense." Panic rippled through her chest. "We need to contact, uh…Rob. Rob Santo. He works with Jace at Connor and Wills. He'll know what's going on."

"Ty already did," Jess said softly.

Emily felt the world shift.

"What do you mean?"

Jess reached for Emily's hand and pursed her lips as if she were about to say something unpleasant. "Rob said Jason quit Thursday morning. Suddenly. Cleaned out his desk and walked out. He's gone, Em. Vanished."

"Excuse me?"

Her mom spoke. "When did he talk to you last? And what did he say the last time he called you?" her mom asked in the same gentle tone she'd used the moment before.

"It was Wednesday—Wednesday night." Emily swallowed, feeling as if something was suddenly *wrong*. "He sounded weird. Said he couldn't talk. He said the next time we'd hold hands on a beach, it would be at our wedding. And that's today. When he got to Mexico."

She caught the tortured look her best friend gave to her mom.

"I thought it was kind of romantic, arriving last minute and not seeing me until he saw me in my wedding dress."

Emily fiddled with her engagement ring.

"He's not coming, is he?"

PRESENT DAY

Salt water heals wounds.

As Emily wiped at the tears slicking her face—tears that had saturated her life the way the summer rain saturated the ground in a good Dixie storm—she glanced once more at the divorce decree crumpled in her hand.

Her tears did nothing to fix the pain of her failed marriage. Her shredded heart. Her hapless life.

But real salt water, the kind that made the air sticky and humid, the kind that someone could submerge themselves in, just might.

Maybe, she thought, *it can heal whatever is broken inside me.*

ONE

Emily stumbled down the jetway as the Florida humidity hit her in the face like a warm, damp rag. She glanced around. Fort Myers airport, more commonly known to tourists as RSW or Southwest Florida Regional, was larger than when she'd last been through it. Perfect, molded plastic chairs, permanently joined to their neighbors at the armrest, lined expansive gates. Pristine, unremarkable gray paint stood in stark contrast with vibrant carpet, also apparently new.

Despite the humidity, Emily smiled and took a deep breath. The air smelled different here, even miles from the beach. It smelled like *home*.

"Em!"

She turned to the sound of the voice. A wave and a soft smile. *Mom.*

Emily made her way over, carry-on bag in tow.

"Welcome home, Em," her mother said, holding her at arm's length for a moment then hugging her. Her mom's patchouli drifted through the air. "It's about time."

"Thanks for picking me up," Emily said.

Today, her mom wore perfectly round pink sunglasses with peacock blue lenses, a tie-dye scarf attempting to tame her wild hair, a voluminous purple skirt, and sandals that had seen better days. Her outfits had become more randomly put together since her dad died nearly a decade ago.

Mentally, Emily tried on a few adjectives to describe her mom's appearance. *My hippie, artsy mom. My patchouli-wearing, Birkenstock-wearing mom. My bohemian, free-thinking mom.*

It was all so very strange.

But whatever it took to keep her mother distracted from her never-ending grief was more than fine with Emily.

They traveled the escalator down to baggage claim to wait for Emily's luggage.

After retrieving two suitcases from the carousel—filled with things she didn't trust the movers with—her mom led them to the parking garage.

"Let's stop for dinner on the way home," she said. "I haven't any clue whether I have food in the house or not. Or if I do, if it's even edible."

Emily chuckled. "Thanks for letting me stay with you until the rest of my stuff gets here," she said. "The movers are saying everything should arrive Tuesday."

"Of course. You can stay as long as you like, you know," her mom said. "What about dinner at Amber House? The menu is almost entirely vegan. The servers even ask if you allow honey in your meal," she said conspiratorially. "They're so careful, it's wonderful."

Her mom paid the airport parking fee at the toll booth and merged onto the highway toward Westshore Beach. Within twenty minutes they were inside Amber House Restaurant and seated at a cozy table on the patio, scanning the choices for dinner as the gulf breeze whispered around them.

"How's your newly minted ex-husband? Utterly devastated? Or celebrating nightly?" her mom asked from behind her menu.

"I love how you think it's okay to ask me that," Emily said with a wry smile.

Her mother huffed a laugh and adjusted herself in her chair. "Well, how is he?"

"Charles is fine. We're both just fine."

"You two were married for nearly four years. How could you both be *just fine?*"

"Mom, look, I know you don't understand because of how much you adored Dad." She reached across the table and took her mom's hands in hers. It was hard to classify her and Charles' parting as anything but a success, despite the dissolution of their marriage and the hurt it caused. "Charles and I are friends. But that's what we were best at— friendship. We should have never gotten married. It was bound to fall apart."

"Some would love to be married to a man like Charles."

"I know, Mom. Just not me." She offered what she hoped was a comforting smile. "I'm okay. Really. Managing the paperwork from the attorneys has been harder than the actual divorce."

"If you say so." Her mom took a long swallow of ice water.

Emily decided to try to change the subject. "I can pick up the key for the townhouse Monday morning."

"About that."

Emily raised an eyebrow.

"The nice, retired couple next door told me that they're going to be putting their cottage on the market in the next couple of months," her mom said. "You could buy it and live next to me. Imagine the possibilities."

Emily wondered just what it would be like living next to the latest hippie version of her mom. She wasn't exactly sure what it would be like to witness the chaos first-hand every day and night. "I signed a six-month lease," she hedged.

"Which I'm sure you could break," her mom said. "Well, I just thought I'd mention it. You know, live next to your aging mother. Make sure I can find the right channel to watch Wheel of Fortune. Make sure I take my old age pills and whatnot."

Emily rolled her eyes. "You don't own a TV, Mom. And I'm sure you don't need me to take care of anything," she said. "You never have."

"What if I can't get the day's wine bottle open?"

"*That's* what you're concerned about?"

"What if a pervert moves in next door? I'll have to pull down my shades or my wrinkled bum will be all over the internet."

Emily laughed.

"So," her mom continued without missing a beat, "have you thought any more about what career you'd like to pursue next?"

"I'm working on that," Emily said. "I know I want a change, but I'm not sure what kind of job I want. I don't want to work in technology for a big corporation anymore. Too much visibility. No more midnight calls when the mail server goes down. I want something completely different." Her belly thrilled with the possibility of it. "I figure I have at least a year before things begin to get critical."

"A year can feel like a very long amount of time." Her mom was silent for a moment. "I need to tell you something, Em. I'm not quite sure how to bring it up, but there's something I think you should know."

Reaching into her voluminous canvas purse, her mom produced a large, glossy postcard and handed it to Emily. The advertisement boasted photographs of a new building with a pristine waiting room and included a coupon for new patients for their first visit. Emily turned it over.

Dr. Jason Williams, DVM, Williams Veterinary Clinic

Emily felt her face heat and her stomach plunge sickeningly. "What is this?"

"It came in the mail yesterday," her mom said. "I realize there's no photo of the man in question and your Jason isn't a vet—"

Emily found her voice. "Jason isn't *mine*," she said.

"Right." Her mom's lips thinned in frustration. "Now that you're back home, advertisements like this one might find their way to your mailbox. I wanted you to be prepared."

"It can't be him. He's not a veterinarian. He's in information technology, like I was."

"But the name, Em."

"Williams is one of the most common surnames in the United States. The chances that he quit his job, went to vet school, and moved to my hometown—of all places—are astronomical. Beyond astronomical, even."

"It's just an odd coincidence from the universe, I guess," her mom conceded. She gestured vaguely as if to dispel bad juju that had settled in the air, her bracelets clicking and clinking together as if in song.

"Exactly," Emily agreed. "Just a coincidence."

"But I'm sure you know, the universe has arranged stranger things than that," her mom said leaning forward.

Emily made a noise halfway between a sigh and a groan. Once her mom was convinced of something, she held onto it. Tightly.

"Why on earth would he move here?" Emily asked, exasperated.

"Sorry to burst your bubble, sweetie, but people can move anywhere they feel like it. I mean, who wouldn't want

15

to live in Westshore Beach?" she asked, waving toward the gulf. "It's not like he hasn't visited here before. If memory serves, you met him here when he was visiting his cousin, Tyler."

"So helpful, Mom."

"Look, what you need is a couple of good days just lying on the prettiest beach in the world. Listening to the waves. Drinking smoothies. And some yoga—you need some yoga. A friend of mine opened a studio and on Tuesday and Thursday mornings they offer goat yoga. Can you believe it? Goat yoga? You should try it. You'd love it."

Her mom held out her hand for the postcard, no doubt to recycle it. Even before her current unbridled hippie phase, one of her mom's life goals was to rid the world of junk mail one postcard at a time.

"If you don't mind, I'm going to hold on to this," Emily said.

Her mom gave her an odd look, then waved the server over to the table to take their orders.

On the drive to the beach cottage, her mom chatted incessantly about her window herb garden and the latest repairs on her beloved VW Beetle.

"Lately I've been thinking of buying an old RV and refurbishing it," her mom said as they turned the final corner onto her street. "I could become a nomad for a year. Live in those Bureau of Land Management open areas. Hang out with the antelope and whatnot."

"Those places don't have water," Emily pointed out.

"True. But if you don't like your neighbors, you can drive away."

As they pulled into the driveway of her mom's cottage, Emily had to admire the tiny home, neatly nestled between a cluster of sea oats and a saw palmetto, directly on the beach. Even though the bungalow wasn't the house she grew up in, it was cheery, welcoming, and cozy.

Inside, eye-popping colors covered every wall. Lemon kitchen cabinets, a scarlet throw rug, teal curtains. It was an odd combination of beach vibe and hippie, with a sparsity to it that matched her mother's newfound desire for minimalist living. Maybe the cottage wasn't the house she grew up in, but somehow, Emily felt like she'd come home.

Her mom bundled Emily into a spare bedroom barely larger than a twin bed and disappeared to meditate on the deck.

Emily opened her suitcase and began to unpack. She didn't have much with her—most of her belongings were arriving with the movers next week, but a handful of the clothes she had brought with her needed to be hung. Pushing aside a large purple tapestry embroidered with phases of the moon functioning as the closet door, Emily uncovered a long canvas garment bag hanging near the back of the closet. She unzipped it.

Emily felt her stomach sink.

A soft blue sundress, the color of a pale summer sky. No tie-dye. No fringe.

Her mother had never toned anything down for anyone, ever.

Except once.

Eight years ago.

Hadn't her mom told her she'd left the dress behind in the hotel in Mexico? Why was it here? Why had her mom kept it? And what else had her mom kept?

Cringing, she let the curtain fall back over the closet

opening and left her clothes folded in her suitcase.

How could a scant few yards of fabric make her feel like she was suddenly numb?

She was over it. She *was*.

It had been a long day traveling. She was tired, that's all.

Exhausted, Emily dropped down on the bed, rolled on her side, and let sleep take her.

TWO

"**D**octor Williams?"

Jason paused writing notes on the patient chart and glanced at his receptionist. Mel's lips were thinned to white.

"Mrs. Selby and her dog are here again." Mel nodded in the direction of the waiting room. "They're on the walk-in side."

This was Jance Selby's third visit this month. The octogenarian would certainly win the Most Attentive Owner prize if Westshore Beach had one. No doubt her dog, Tootles, slept seventeen minutes later than usual or left a single kibble in his assuredly personalized bowl.

But despite her fiery eyes and abrasive manner—and an ever-present cane that she could likely wield as a weapon—Jason believed, underneath it all, that Mrs. Selby was kind.

And extremely lonely.

"It's fine, Mel. Put her in Exam Room Two. I'll be there within five." He chanced a look around the doorway into the waiting room. As always, the elderly woman was meticulously dressed. Gloves. Pearls. Patent leather shoes. Everything—head to toe—in her customary peach color.

The Queen of England had nothing on this lady.

If her frown and an exasperated huff—directed at no one in particular—were anything to go by, Mrs. Selby seemed extraordinarily agitated.

He winced. "Make that three."

Moments later, Jason opened the door to the exam room, donning his best smile.

Mrs. Selby inspected him from underneath a straw hat adorned with a single plastic rose.

"How are you this morning, Mrs. Selby?" he asked.

Mrs. Selby sat down, pressing the pleats of her skirt until they were arranged perfectly, and brushed lint—or imaginary crumbs—off them. "I am well. But Tootles seems a bit under the weather. He didn't drink all of his water this morning. He receives precisely eight ounces of water at seven o'clock every morning. He drank as he usually does, precisely on time, but walked away without finishing. I measured what was left." She produced a Tupperware container from the depths of her voluminous purse. "Just over three and a half ounces!"

Mrs. Selby's Pomeranian surveyed Jason imperiously as he waited for a diagnosis.

"Any changes in his appetite?"

"None."

"Any coughing, sneezing, excessive panting, or labored breathing?"

"I should hope not," she said indignantly.

Jason finished the examination and gave the dog a pat and a small treat from the room's cookie jar.

"Tootles seems to be fine, Mrs. Selby. I recommend keeping an eye on his behavior, as I'm certain you always do. If you see anything out of the ordinary, just give us a call."

"Very well. Thank you, Doctor Williams."

Jason patted her arm gently. "Anytime you need us, we're

here."

Mrs. Selby shuffled out the door with her Pomeranian in tow, and the office staff seemed to breathe a sigh of relief as if they had dodged a particularly dangerous bullet.

"You have a way with her. Calms her right down," Mel said as Jason returned to the reception area to review the appointments for the rest of the day.

"Sometimes a friendly face is all someone needs. Some of our older clients have no one but their pets. Their dog or cat connects them to life, in a very real way."

Mel gave him an odd look.

The office manager, Kathleen, reappeared from the backroom to join the conversation. "Maybe I should let you handle the phone when she calls. I hear she's burned through every other clinic in the county. We are the last place that will take her."

Jason smiled. "I'm happy to. I think Mrs. Selby is sweet."

"I just figured out what to get you for Christmas," Kathleen said. "A dictionary. Because you haven't any idea what the word 'sweet' means."

"Before I forget," Mel said. "I'd like to ask for next Friday off. Theo and I are planning a long weekend…" She trailed off with a faraway look and a wistful smile, and something under Jason's ribs clenched.

"I assume Callie can cover for you?" Jason asked levelly.

"Yes. I already asked."

"Absolutely. Have a great time."

Mel scampered toward the back room as Kathleen slid into the front desk chair. She leaned toward him and lowered her voice. "You know, you haven't taken a day off in months. Scratch that. I've never seen you take a day off."

They'd had this conversation more times than Jason cared to remember. Kathleen was as competent as they came, but occasionally she took a keen interest in how he spent his time outside his practice. She meant well, but it grated on his nerves.

"Well, I'm still trying to establish the clinic. Ensure things run smoothly."

"That's what you have me for." She smiled. "How about Saturday? You could have the whole weekend. Do something fun. Maybe go to the beach, even."

The front door opened, admitting Mel's cousin, Callie, who worked at the clinic part-time. "Hey, Kathleen. Hello, Doctor Williams."

Even though Callie wasn't his type—not to mention she was engaged to a deployed Marine—there was no denying Callie was cute, curvy, bubbly, and full of life. A light in his current sea of darkness.

"Hi, Callie. I've asked you a million times, call me Jason."

She leaned close enough for him to smell her perfume and said conspiratorially, "Okay. Just not while I'm here."

"Compelled to come in even on your day off," Jason said.

"It just so happens that our clinic is the most exciting place in Westshore Beach. No one can stay away." She giggled. "Even so, I'm here to grab lunch with Mel."

Kathleen piped up. "I was just trying to convince Doctor Williams to take a day off and go out for an evening. Relax a little."

"I can't take a Saturday off. Often, it's our busiest day," he said.

"A Monday or Tuesday, then."

"I'm sure we already have appointments on the books."

"Yes, but—"

"You know what?" Callie said. "My fiancé said the same thing to me today. He said…" Callie lowered her voice theatrically in a decent mimicry of a man's voice. "You should go out with the girls for drinks. Let your hair down. Have a good time." She looked at Jason pointedly. "Why don't you come out with Mel and me sometime? We like to go to Gulf and Main. Ever been there?"

"I know where it is," Jason said cautiously.

"It's settled then," Callie said with a bright smile. "Next week. I'll let you know which day."

"I—" Jason began, but Callie had already walked away.

Kathleen shook her head. "That was the best assumptive close I've seen in a while," she said. "I should have tried that on you myself."

THREE

"You do realize Mom's beach cottage is *on the beach*, right?"

"Yep," Jess said. "I got that."

Five minutes before, Jess, Emily's best friend since high school, had pulled up in her battered car, bikini peeking out from underneath her cutoff shorts, her long brown hair in a ponytail. When the chairs and beach bags had been loaded— the hatchback groaning in protest as Jess slammed it shut— Emily climbed in the passenger seat and yanked her door closed. Sand had bounced out of every crack and crevice in the entire car.

"Maybe we don't even need to go to the beach," she'd said, brushing the sand off her thigh. "We could just open the sunroof and sit here."

Her best friend had grunted a laugh and wrenched the shift into first gear, and the ancient Toyota lurched forward as the traffic light turned green.

"You could leave your car in the driveway, and we could eat lunch inside," Emily continued, "in the air conditioning. Mom's not even home right now—she's at her guided meditation group." Emily pointed to the next corner. "You can make a U-turn at Eighth Street."

"Nope." Jess shook her head, her ponytail whipping into the driver's side window. "Not on a Monday."

"Okay, fine." Emily sighed. "But I don't understand why we have to be there so early."

"Trust me. We want to get to South Cove before noon. *You* want to get to South Cove before noon."

The traffic light turned red, and Jess urged the car to a rolling stop.

"I don't even think we went there once in high school," Emily said.

"You're right." Her best friend tossed her a sly smile. "It's different now. Much more exciting. You'll see why when we get there."

"So much mystery."

"It will be obvious, I promise," Jess said. "Seeing is believing."

"Okay," Emily said after a moment. "So, how were the fifth graders this year?"

"Great, as always," Jess said. "We've got a new principal starting in the fall. I met him two weeks before the end of last semester. Moved here from Georgia. Seems like a good fit, but I guess we'll see." The car swerved, avoiding a pothole. "When does the rest of your stuff arrive?"

"All the boxes and furniture should be delivered Tuesday, but my car won't be here until next week." They turned onto West Gulf Road. "When are you coming over to see my new place?"

"How about Friday?"

"Sure."

"We should swing by The Pub at Gulf and Main for a drink soon," Jess said. "I don't think it was open the last time you were home."

"Okay." Emily turned to watch the houses slide by. "That'll be fun. Charles and I never went out. He was always too tired when he was a resident, and once he took his boards, he was too busy. Complaining about it seemed selfish. Eventually, I just learned to live the life we had, thinking we'd have time for it eventually. I never stopped wanting to go out, though."

"You, my friend, are far too young to stay at home every night," Jess said, peering at Emily over her sunglasses.

"I'm old enough to stay home most nights, though."

"Ain't nobody old enough for that."

After a moment, Emily said, "I need a favor, Jess."

"Name it."

"You know how I have this thing with schedules and routine? I…um…I need to get over it. It's gotten a lot worse lately with the divorce. I need to, I don't know, ease off on the habitual stuff."

"Calculated reckless abandon, here we come."

"I'm looking for *spontaneity*, Jess."

"Done and done, my friend."

Seventeen minutes later, Jess eased her car into one of the last unoccupied spaces in the South Cove parking lot. The driver's door screeched as Jess slid out to open the rear hatch and drag their chairs and beach bags onto the asphalt.

"Crowded today. The word is out," Jess muttered as she handed Emily her bag.

"Looks like nearly all of the spaces are resident only," Emily said.

"Yeah. Most of Westshore Beach is like that now. I'd get your car registered in Florida as soon as you can. I wouldn't even attempt parking without a resident beach sticker in winter, and it's easier to park at South Cove on Mondays if you have one. I'm sure," she said with another coy smile, "it's because of the view."

"The view isn't different here than—"

Jess nodded toward Emily's book. "Em, it's *Monday*. You're not gonna need that. Trust."

They made their way to the boardwalk connecting the parking lot to the beach. The cloudless sky was a washed-out blue, promising a stifling afternoon. Thankful for the gulf breeze, Emily kicked off her flip-flops the moment her toes hit the sand.

"Right there," Jess said, pointing at a nondescript patch of unoccupied sand to their right. "It's the best spot. I've tried them all, and this angle is best."

Two permanently installed aluminum poles stood innocently about five yards away.

Emily groaned. "Seriously, Jess? You brought me here to watch beach volleyball? What, are we in high school?"

"You'll thank me later," Jess whispered back.

A moment later, two guys sauntered up to the sand court, dropped armloads of equipment into a pile, and began stretching a volleyball net between the poles. The taller of the two peeled off his shirt in the way that muscled men do: with arms crossed and fabric stretched to its limit.

Holy hell.

"Oh," Emily whispered, feeling a bit envious of the shirt.

"Yeah," Jess whispered back. "Just wait. They haven't even started yet."

One of the guys dug around in a duffle bag until he found the guidewires, and together the two of them unrolled the rope and anchored it to the poles. A couple more guys jogged up and, after shaking hands with the others, unpacked three volleyballs.

Emily sighed. "Do they have a physical requirement to earn a position on the team? Because *damn*."

"Right?" Jess said, unfolding her chair. "Like, how in the hell are they all that gorgeous?" She sat down, keeping her eyes on the makeshift court. "Truth is, I think they all know each other from the gym."

"How did you find out about it?" Emily asked.

Her best friend hesitated, face flushing. "Well...uh..." Then she snapped her mouth shut.

Emily raised an eyebrow until Jess relented.

"Ty told me about it. Sometimes he plays with the rest of the guys. When he's in town and done processing his latest raw images, that is."

Tyler—Jace's cousin. The man who'd introduced Emily to Jace eight and a half years ago.

"Look, you don't have to worry, Em. Ty's in Africa right now. As we speak, he's probably snapping a gazillion photos of a cheetah chasing down a poor zebra for its next meal. Or watching elephants roll around in the mud. You won't see him today. I wouldn't spring that on you, I promise."

Emily nodded. She knew she'd bump into Tyler sooner or later—it was just another one of those things she'd have to accept if she was going to live in Westshore Beach permanently. But Tyler playing beach volleyball? It didn't compute. Despite his penchant for leaving the continent to take photos of wild animals, Tyler seemed more comfortable in a cowboy hat and boots, than in flip flops and board shorts.

Not that seeing Tyler would be bad if he looks half as good as the rest of these guys do.

"Here's a few more," Jess murmured as more deliciously tan and muscled guys sauntered up and greeted the rest, shaking hands and nodding while assessing the competition. "Oh, you're in for a treat. That dark-haired guy is—"

"No way. Nuh-uh. Nope."

"Yup. Mike Malone. Westshore Beach High."

Mike peeled off a threadbare, faded concert t-shirt revealing ridiculous abs and a delicious L-shaped indentation pointing downward—

Wow, it's been a long time if you're having thoughts like that about Mike Malone.

"Damn." Emily shook her head. "He looks a bit different than when I saw him last."

The guys finished anchoring the net.

"They'll start with a warmup of setting and serving," Jess said. "I studied up on beach volleyball terms and rules. Because," she said, leaning closer to Emily, "it'll come in handy one day soon, I'm certain of it."

The game's first serve arched wide, and the volleyball rolled toward Emily and Jess. Her best friend jumped out of her beach chair, retrieved it, and tossed it to a guy with a ponytail waiting at the edge of the sand court. He winked at Jess and thanked her for retrieving the ball.

"I think they're beginning to remember me," she whispered after sitting back down in her chair.

"Do you think that's a good thing?"

"I *know* it's a good thing."

Emily laughed, eyes on the game. "Talk to me about something mundane. Something. Anything. Because *damn*," she muttered.

"Remind me what the word mundane means."

"You're the teacher, Jess."

"I seemed to have left my dictionary…somewhere other than here."

"Let's talk about getting my car's oil changed. That seems pretty mundane."

"Except if one of these guys changes your oil," Jess whispered.

"You, my friend, have a filthy mind."

"Uh-huh," Jess said as one of the guys dove to the ground for a save. "Maybe we should get something cold to drink. Or ice cream."

"I think we're going to need an entire ice cream truck."

Mike turned and winked at Emily before smacking the ball over the net for a point.

"Dude, you're in town for approximately twenty seconds and men are staring," Jess said. "I call unsportsmanlike conduct."

"I'm sure Mike recognizes me from high school, that's all."

"Uh-huh."

Within half an hour, seven guys with rippling muscles were taking turns on the sand court. And for Emily, there was something about sitting in a beach chair, staring at bronzed skin and hard muscles, that was absolutely, unequivocally perfect.

Emily watched the movers lugging in box after cardboard box from the truck in her driveway, hefting the heaviest—ones she'd marked *BOOKS* with a fat, black marker when she'd packed them, weeks ago—into the family room and stacking them against the pristine wall.

One of the men caught her stare and smirked. She wondered what his bicep would feel against her—

She shook the thought away.

Wow, first the volleyball players, now the movers. Get a grip, Emily.

Maybe he flexed a bit more when he brought in the next box filled with books.

Just *maybe.*

Emily felt her face color and turned to the window, taking a sip of coffee, long cold. Yesterday afternoon at South Cove Beach reminded her of how long it had been since she had woken up next to someone.

One of the movers placed a carton on top of one of the stacks against the far wall. "This is the last of it," he said, handing Emily paperwork to sign with a cocky smile. "If you need anything else, don't hesitate to call."

I could use some help getting the squeaks out of my bed, she thought. *I'd need you for a test drive or two.*

"Thanks," she mumbled as they left.

Wandering around the dining room, she noticed a lone carton sitting in the corner on the floor. Emily was well acquainted with that particular box. It had huddled, sealed and out of sight, in the back of her closet for eight years—except for a recent unearthing when she added a few more things—but she knew exactly what lay hidden inside.

Relics of heartbreak.

Having the moving company pack it with her other boxes took more courage than she'd anticipated.

I should have paid them to lose it instead.

Eight years ago, on her best friend's advice, she'd packed everything that Jace had left behind—including her engagement ring—and sealed it in the box. It had been nearly a decade since she'd stuffed it behind a carton of college notebooks in the back of her closet, and now it had invaded her new home like a raincloud.

The crushing loss. The abandonment. Everything had seemed easier to handle when the box remained out of sight.

The sight of it now made her miss Jace even more than usual.

It's ridiculous to miss someone who shattered your heart the way he did, she reminded herself. *There's no way you can long for someone who did that. It makes no sense at all.*

Her best friend didn't understand it, either. The last time Jess had visited, she'd seen the box—quite by accident—when she'd been rummaging around in Emily's closet for a pair of shoes to wear to dinner.

"I can't believe you still have that. It's been long enough, Em. Toss it out without opening it," Jess had said. "Stop torturing yourself."

Emily had refused.

So here it was, staring at her from the corner of the dining room in her new townhouse, thousands of miles from where she'd been, whispering reminders of disastrous engagements and failed marriages.

I wonder if my wedding ring from Charles is keeping the engagement ring from Jace company? I bet they're best buds.

With a bitter huff, Emily turned away and wandered back to the living room.

Her couch had been Saran-wrapped within an inch of its life. She found a utility knife and cut the plastic away from it, freeing the pillows, and peeled off her socks, dropping down into the cushions with a grateful sigh.

The townhouse was thick with silence.

Her thoughts turned to her ex-husband.

As much as she suggested to her mom that her relationship with Charles remained fundamentally sound, there was certainly lingering hurt. Lost expectations. Time squandered on things that didn't work out. Even the simple loss of his constant presence—since she was a *spending time* love language kind of person—chafed.

She and Charles had been comfortable. It—*they*—had always been, well, comfortable. And now they remained comfortable...friends.

The chain of events that pushed their relationship over the edge didn't matter. The divorce had been the best thing for both of them. Best for the future. Best in the long view.

Even if it did sting a bit.

She was thankful that one of the many things that Charles was good at—maybe the only thing that mattered at this point—was investing money. The abundance of cash in Emily's bank account after the divorce had given her a cushion of time to decide what she wanted to do next. It had been an unexpected benefit, and one she was determined to take advantage of.

But right now, the only thing Emily knew for certain was that she didn't want to go back to the same kind of job she'd had in Virginia.

There wasn't anything like her old job available in Westshore Beach anyway. Most careers in her hometown were in tourism, medicine, or banking. She wasn't qualified to do any of that.

Well, not yet. Things could be very different in a year.

Emily dragged her laptop onto the couch next to her and pried it open. What should she search for? What would be the best career for someone newly single, with a penchant for warm climates, lost causes, vegan food, and schedules carved in stone?

Nothing. Absolutely…nothing.

Folding herself deeper into the couch, she surveyed the moving boxes standing around the room in perfect stacks like cardboard soldiers. Too much to deal with. Tonight, she'd unpack her television and Roku, and cozy up with some Netflix and a hefty glass of Scotch. By any stretch, a lofty goal after a seemingly endless day.

As Jess was fond of saying, recharging your batteries was as easy as sliced cheese.

FOUR

The townhouse was simply too quiet.

Yawning, Emily tossed the sheets off her bed and padded to the window, opening it to the swampy air and the din of a Florida summer night. Darkness pressed in, but the drone of the air conditioner, the chorus of frogs, and the enthusiastic song of the cicadas did nothing to temper the emptiness.

Even a raucous summer night could feel utterly empty.

Much to her mom's dismay, Emily had leased the townhouse sight unseen, telling herself that the unremarkable rental would be fine until she found something to buy closer to the beach and more her style. Although she didn't own it, for the next six months it was hers, and hers alone. And for that, she was thankful.

The air conditioner clicked off, and the frogs and cicadas followed suit.

Silence.

A dog barked down the street, interrupting the leaden quiet, and, despite the hour, she smiled. Emily loved dogs. When she was a kid, her mom and dad had always owned at least two, big as bears.

A second bark reminded her of how much her ex-husband disliked dogs, and how she'd finally given up pleading for a puppy during the difficult years of his residency. Dogs had been just another thing missing from the life she had tried so desperately to make work.

"With you at the hospital so much, I'm alone most of the time," Emily argued. *"I need company."*

"Since I am hardly ever home," Charles said, exasperation hardening the lines of his face, *"the last thing I'd want to do is take care of yet another thing when I'm here. All I want to do when I get home is sleep."*

"I know you're exhausted every moment of every day," she said. *"I'd never ask you to take care of a puppy. I'll do everything. I'm lonely, Charles. You're never here—"*

"You knew what my residency would be like, Emily."

"But—"

"I'm tired," he said, turning away. *"And this conversation is over."*

Wincing at the memory, Emily closed the window and wandered back to bed. Charles wasn't a difficult man, necessarily. He simply had strong opinions.

About everything.

But Jace loved dogs—they'd planned on adopting at least one puppy when they got back from Cancún.

Emily chuckled, nodding in the direction of a little boy and his puppy, who had suddenly decided he was too tired to continue walking on his leash through Bristol Park. The dog plopped down, back legs splaying, the sides of his round belly spilling out over the sidewalk.

She glanced at Jace.

"When we get back," he said, lacing his fingers in hers. *"After we're married. As many dogs as you want."*

"When we get back," Emily agreed.

As she laid back down in bed, she wondered when every sound and thought wouldn't trace back to the man who abandoned her eight years ago.

Maybe, she thought, snuggling deeper into the sheets, *one way to make that memory sting a little less would be to get a dog of my own.*

"I rarely use the car anymore," her mom said, dropping a set of keys in Emily's palm. "I prefer to walk or take my bike. Keep it until yours arrives."

"If you're sure..."

Her mom waved her off with a smile and retreated behind her easel on the deck, blue and purple paint already leaving a trail the color of twilight along her chin and in her hair.

Her mom's Volkswagen Beetle fired up in a gust of black smoke, shuddering violently. Emily backed out of the driveway, wondering when her mom had changed the oil last. As she passed the edge of Westshore Beach, Emily struggled to keep the car from veering off the road as it twisted through the Florida slash pine standing thick as far as she could see.

Better tell mom to get this hunk of junk aligned. Like, yesterday.

The crocheted peace sign swinging despondently from the rear-view mirror seemed to nod in agreement.

A few miles later, she arrived.

Westshore Beach's no-kill dog shelter turned out to be a single-story building with large windows stretching across the brick front face. The parking lot was empty, and the sign on the door announced that the shelter didn't open until nine.

Exciting, she thought sarcastically as she stalked back to the car to wait. *I've made it big,* she thought, climbing back into her mom's Beetle. *Reduced to sitting in an empty parking lot on a Tuesday morning with no coffee, deleting junk mail on my cell.*

Within a couple of minutes, a truck pulled into the lot and a woman stepped out, glancing Emily's way.

"We're not open for another fifteen minutes," she called.

Emily returned to scrolling through the long list of unread mail in her inbox.

Halfway to the door, the woman turned around and walked back toward Emily's car. "Are you here to adopt?"

She nodded. "Yes, I am."

"How about you come in and meet some of our residents while I boot up the computers," the woman said.

The volunteer—Allison, according to her nametag—unlocked the door, shouldered it open with a grunt, and shuffled her way behind the reception desk to deposit her belongings.

"Which dog has been here the longest?" Emily asked as the woman finished powering up the near-obsolete desktops.

"A little mixed breed, right down this way," Allison said. "We don't know for certain, but we think he's the oldest dog here as well."

Emily followed the volunteer down a cement hallway, bordered on both sides by chain link fence gates, confining hopeful, wagging tales and sleepy eyes.

"Here he is," Allison said, pointing at the pen just ahead of them. The little black and brown dog leaned against the fence separating him from the cage to his right. His eyes followed Emily as she approached his run, his bottom wiggling faster and faster as she got closer.

"I'm surprised he's been here this long," the volunteer said. "He's very sweet. He's just not…"

The little dog waddled to the front of the pen and gazed up at Emily. Several bottom teeth protruded from his mouth at a disturbing angle. Drool pooled onto his lips, and then his chin.

But he was smiling.

"...what someone envisions when they think of bringing home a dog for the family," Emily supplied.

"Maybe." Allison met Emily's eye. "He's up to date on his vaccinations—as all our residents are—but we always suggest a visit to your vet within a week of adoption, just to establish a baseline of health."

"Do you have a recommendation?"

"We use Beach County Animal Hospital. They take care of all the dogs here gratis. Snaggles actually loves going to the vet."

"Snaggles?"

She nodded at the cage. "The volunteers call this little guy Snaggles—short for Snaggletooth. He has a bit of an overbite in his bottom jaw."

Emily looked down at the dog's weepy eyes. Saliva dripped from his chin onto the cement floor.

"Right," Emily said.

"Older dogs take a lot of time, a lot of patience, and sometimes, a lot of money to care for," Allison said levelly.

"Don't we all."

The volunteer gave her a wry smile. "True."

Emily bent down to say hello, and Snaggles waddled closer to the chain-link gate.

Allison said, "Why don't you take him around the grounds for a minute? He's great on a leash. Just make sure you keep him on it. He's a bit of an escape artist when he's off a lead."

The volunteer opened the gate and Emily secured the

leash on the little dog's collar. If anything, his tail beat faster. When she led him out the back door of the shelter and into a fenced area, he smiled even wider.

"What do you think, Snaggles? You and me? Partners in crime?" Emily asked.

They wandered around the back of the cement path lined with live oak, saw palmetto, and slash pine. "See, to anyone else, it looks like we're down on our luck. But just because someone's divorced, or someone's in a shelter, that doesn't mean they actually *are* down on their luck."

Snaggles glanced up at her.

"We're not, now, are we? All we need is a second chance. New beginnings and all that. You'd like that, wouldn't you? A second chance?"

The little dog plodded alongside her, looking up every so often with a wide doggie smile.

"You're a pretty good listener, aren't you, little guy?"

Allison was waiting for them halfway back to the main building. "What do you think?"

Emily looked down at the little dog. A string of stickiness dripped from his snout onto the sidewalk. "I think Snaggles found a new home."

The first thing Emily did when she got home with Snaggles was call Jess.

"I just got home from the dog shelter," she said.

"You got a puppy?" Jess asked.

Emily glanced at the tiny, drooling beast with his gray snout and cloudy eyes, exhausted from the day's excitement, and curled up on the dog bed she'd purchased on their way home. "Not exactly."

"I'll be right over."

While Jess was on her way, Emily found the postcard her mom received in the mail from the veterinary clinic, double-checking to ensure the one listed on the card wasn't the same one the shelter had recommended. It wasn't.

Emily had no desire to hear the name *Jason Williams*, even if it wasn't *her* Jason Williams, thank-you-very-much.

Besides, Jason Disappearing-Act Williams had never really been hers anyway, right?

Right.

"May I put you on hold?" the Beach County Animal Hospital receptionist asked after Emily explained that she'd adopted a dog that morning and wanted to make an appointment.

She paced the living room, surveying what seemed to be an insurmountable number of boxes to unpack while Snaggles twitched as if he were chasing a particularly nimble rabbit in his dreams.

The receptionist's voice came back on the line. "Thanks for your patience."

"No problem," Emily said.

"Things have been crazy today," the receptionist continued. "One of our doctors had to leave town for a few days due to a family emergency and we're working on covering her appointments. We happen to have an opening at 11:45 tomorrow due to a cancellation. Otherwise, the next opening isn't until Tuesday the 24th at three."

Jess opened Emily's front door and plopped down on the couch, nearly spilling her iced coffee. A donut covered with pink icing and sprinkles stuck out of her mouth. Emily cringed.

"Tomorrow at 11:45 will work." Emily silently offered her best friend a napkin to place underneath her drink before she set it on the side table. "My name is Emily Driscoll," she said to the receptionist.

After Emily hung up, Jess glanced at her. "I thought you were going to stop using Driscoll."

Emily shrugged. "It's automatic, I guess. It doesn't mean anything." Sighing, she said, "I guess it never did."

"I like the townhouse." Jess took a long swallow of her iced coffee. "And before I forget, it seems like the front gate won't stay closed. Something's wrong with the latch," she said.

"Thanks. I'll let them know," Emily said.

Jess glanced around. "So, where's the new doggie?"

FIVE

"**D**octor Williams? I've got Beach County on hold. One of the doctors was called out of town on an emergency. They'd like to know if you can cover appointments tomorrow morning and Friday afternoon."

Kathleen swiveled her chair to face Jason, her eyebrows raised in question.

Williams Veterinary Clinic's reciprocal relationship with Beach County Animal Hospital seemed both a blessing and a curse. Since Jason was the only doctor at Williams currently, his fledgling clinic needed coverage should there be an emergency while he was out of town. Not that Jason could imagine an occasion where he *would* be out of town—but still, he refused to leave his patients without backup emergency care. Nevertheless, covering at Beach County could sometimes be a bit of a chore.

"What's tomorrow morning look like?" Jason asked.

"One surgery at 8. Then nothing until 1:00," Kathleen said.

"Sure. Let them know I can arrive around 9:30."

"Will do."

"And let them know I can be there after 1 p.m. on Friday," Jason added.

The front doorbell sounded and a woman with blonde hair and striking, full-sleeve tattoos strode in. She glanced around and headed for the front desk, brown and black rottweiler in tow.

"Is this the walk-in clinic?" she asked tentatively.

Jason answered from behind the desk. "Yes. I'm Doctor Williams. How can I help you?"

"Bear has been retching on and off for around half an hour. Nothing's coming out," she said. "And he seems off. Pacing. He won't sit down."

"Come on back. Let's take a look."

Once they were settled in the room, Jason started his examination. Bear coughed. Feeling the dog's stomach, Jason asked, "When did Bear last eat?"

"Maybe 40 minutes ago, now? Maybe 45?"

"Did anything unusual happen right after he ate?"

The woman frowned. "Well, right when he finished his breakfast, he took off at a dead run after a squirrel. Next thing I know, he comes back on the deck and won't stop coughing and drooling and trying to throw up."

Jason opened the door to the back and called, "Callie? I need you to get prepped."

He turned back to the owner, who had gone a bit pale. "What's your name?"

"Cassidy Norwich."

"Cassidy, it looks like Bear has something we call GDV or bloat. Do you know what that is?"

The woman nodded and crossed her arms, running her hands up and down her tattoos as if the room had suddenly become cold. "His stomach is twisted."

"That's right. He's going to need surgery, as soon as

possible."

"Is he going to be okay?" Cassidy asked in a shaky voice.

"You got him here fast, and that's a very good thing," Jason said. Callie, his vet tech, appeared with a collapsible gurney. "As soon as I have any information, I'll let you know."

The three of them helped Bear onto it and Cassidy kissed the top of the dog's head. "It's okay, Bear-Bear. You're gonna be just fine."

A tear slipped out her eye.

As he wheeled the dog down to the operating room, Jason motioned for Kathleen to follow.

"The walk-in in exam room one has GDV," he said to her. "The owner's name is Cassidy. Answer her questions. Get her a bottle of water and sit with her to make sure she's okay."

Snaggles loved riding in the car.

The little drooling dog sat upright in the passenger seat of Emily's mom's Volkswagen quivering with excitement as they sped down Gulf Drive, the simple joy in his eyes warming Emily's heart.

Admittedly, Emily needed the lift. She'd awoken from a nightmare around 6 a.m., opening her eyes to find Snaggles curled up next to her, snout on her leg as if he were trying his best to comfort her.

Weary, she'd gotten out of bed and wandered to the bathroom. Emily hated those dreams. In them she was always waiting for someone; sometimes it was her dad. Other times, it was Jace.

Neither ever showed up no matter how long she waited.

Wandering into the kitchen, she'd noticed the postcard

her mom had saved for her—the one advertising Williams Veterinary Clinic—sitting innocently on the counter.

How was she going to live in Westshore if just the mention of his name sent her mind careening in the wrong direction and her dreams spiraling into nightmares?

After taking Snaggles out in the backyard, she'd crawled back under the covers, but sleep refused to come. Sometime later, she'd dragged herself out of bed, made herself coffee, and got ready to go to Snaggles' appointment.

At least the old dog adored car rides.

Once at the clinic, a vet tech led Emily into a depressingly ordinary beige exam room and typed in Snaggles' information on a computer mounted on a rolling cart.

"The doctor will be with you shortly," the tech said with a smile and opened the door, disappearing into the back.

Easy laughter drifted in.

For a breath, the laughter flowed over her like honey, sweet and warm—*and familiar.*

Emily blinked.

The door clicked shut.

Through the wall, she could hear a muffled voice.

She hadn't heard it in more than eight years, but it was the same voice that had invaded her dreams the night before.

A voice she would know anywhere.

Her stomach sank and she felt her face heat.

No—

She had barely formed the rest of her thought when the veterinarian entered, the woman's greeting drowning out all the other voices. "Hello. I'm Doctor Strom."

Great. After that stupid dream, I'm imagining his voice everywhere.

Emily did her best to smile. "I'm Emily Driscoll."

"Well, hello, Snaggles. Remember me?" the vet asked as she bent down to greet the dog. "I can't tell you how thrilled

I am to see that he's been adopted. He's such a sweet little guy, and he's in great shape for his age," she continued, listening to his heart and checking his mouth and eyes. "The only thing I'd recommend right now is a teeth cleaning."

"When could we do it?"

"If I can keep him now, we'll have him back to you tomorrow afternoon."

"Okay," Emily agreed, a twinge of reluctance creeping across her skin.

Doctor Strom noticed. "He'll be absolutely fine," she said with a reassuring smile.

"I just don't want him thinking I'm abandoning him. I just adopted him yesterday."

"Getting his teeth cleaned will help him stay healthier longer, which means Snaggles will get to spend more healthy and happy years with you."

Emily bent to plant a kiss on the Snaggle's head. "I'll see you tomorrow, little guy."

Emily was unlocking her front door when her cell buzzed.

"Hey, Jess."

"Hey, yourself." Jess's cheery voice bounced around the kitchen as Emily busied herself with making a salad for lunch.

"So, how about we go out for drinks tonight? Celebrate your move home?"

"Tonight?" Emily asked wearily, suppressing a yawn. "I have so much unpacking to do. There are so many boxes, I don't even know where to start."

"Come on, Em, it's exactly what you need. It's not like the boxes are in danger of toppling over and crushing you. They're not going anywhere," Jess said.

"And they won't be going anywhere until I unpack them. I've only unpacked the glassware so far."

"When was the last time we went out? It's Thursday, Em! You can't sit home."

"Exactly. It's *Thursday*."

"Half-price apps and margaritas at Gulf and Main, every Thursday, four to six," Jess said, sounding every bit a radio promotion.

Emily rolled her eyes.

"Come on, Em," Jess pleaded. "Spontaneous, remember?"

Taking a deep breath, Emily looked around. She still wasn't in the mood to unpack, and the townhouse was even more silent without Snaggles there—without him breathing through crooked teeth—a sound she'd already become used to.

The memory surfaced—of the voice drifting in from the back room at the veterinary clinic. That was all she needed to change her mind.

"Okay," Emily said. "But one drink and we leave."

The Pub at Gulf and Main had opened sometime after Emily had relocated to Virginia with Charles, and it was obviously the hottest place to be in Westshore Beach on a Thursday night. Most of the tables and barstools were full, and tonight, a blues band played from the corner on the other side of a small wooden dance floor.

"Sometimes I feel like this is the only place in town," Jess muttered, glancing around, her eyes snagging on a guy halfway down the bar. "Not that I'm complaining."

The bartender was a short woman with sandy blonde hair,

perfect brows and lips, gorgeous tattoos, and a knowing smile. "What'll it be?" she asked as they climbed into two barstools, a suggestion of a southern accent infusing her words.

"Two margaritas and a menu," Jess said. The bartender produced two premade drinks in plastic cups from a row behind her. Three guys standing down the bar turned to glance their way.

"They're circling like sharks around a shiny new toy," Jess whispered.

"I think you're mixing your metaphors. Besides, I don't want to be a toy, and I certainly don't want to be eaten by a shark."

Jess waggled her eyebrows. "You sure?" she asked before taking a sip of her margarita.

"Jess! I can't imagine—"

"Emily? Emily Lanson?"

She glanced up to meet the striking blue eyes of a man with a deliciously sharp jawline and thick, dark hair.

"It *is* you!" he said. "I thought it was you at the beach the other day. It's Mike Malone. Westshore High. It's been ages. How are you?"

Emily stumbled. "Wow. Mike. How are you?" Mike somehow looked even taller standing next to her table than he did at the beach. His t-shirt strained across a muscular chest. She pictured his tanned skin and abs on display at the volleyball game and felt her face heat.

"Last I knew you went to college in Chicago." He shifted on his feet and cocked his head to the side as he watched her, assessing. It was a bit unnerving, if she were being honest.

"I did. You went to Gainesville, right?" Emily said, trying hard to get her composure back.

"Yeah. How long are you in town?" he said.

"Actually, I moved back last week. Permanently." She looked to her best friend. Unfortunately, Jess was gaping, lips parted in surprise. "You remember Jessie?"

"Sure," he said with a brief nod in Jess's direction. Focusing back on Emily, he said, "Maybe we could have coffee sometime. Maybe a drink?" He produced a napkin from his pocket and thrust it toward her. "Here's my number. Give me a call or text or whatever," he said with a stunning smile and turned away to stroll back to his buddies.

Emily felt her eyes widen as she watched him walk away. "What just happened?"

Jess snickered. "Looks like you have another reason to ignore those boxes. An absolutely drop-dead gorgeous, six-foot, two-inch reason who apparently kept his number on a piece of paper in his pocket just in case he ran into you."

SIX

Beach County Animal Hospital was much too busy for Jason's comfort. Sure, it was fine to fill in as needed occasionally, to reinforce the *I'll-scratch-your-back-and-you-scratch-mine* kind of relationship for his fledgling practice. But this flurry of activity, today, was a bit much.

Jason's favorite part of his new career as a veterinarian, of course, was helping injured or sick animals, like Cassidy's Rottweiler, Bear, who had luckily arrived at the clinic before too much internal damage had been done. But Jason also loved taking his time with his patients. He wanted to get to know people and their animals, develop relationships, and keep the interactions friendly and casual. There was no time for any of that here. Whenever he filled in at the biggest, oldest, and most established clinic in the area, he felt like a tiny cog in a giant wheel.

And he hated it.

It was Jason's second day covering for a doctor who had to leave unexpectedly for a family emergency. He'd worked at his own clinic until noon and grabbed a quick lunch on the way, and now, Jason was in the middle of the typical hustle of a Friday afternoon at the county's largest veterinary hospital.

Admittedly, Beach County Animal Hospital had

advantages over his clinic. A dedicated operating room for dental procedures. Another for laser surgery. And admittedly, he'd always been a bit envious of their technology, with more than a dozen laptops on tall, wheeled carts, and every single patient record available digitally.

But Jason knew computers, and he knew it was one more reason for the distance between patients and doctors here.

Sighing, he stepped into the hallway connecting the hospital's fifteen exam rooms.

An anonymous tech shoved a computer cart toward him and bolted toward the kennel. The record indicated Jason's next patient had spent the night recovering from a routine procedure and, even though the dog was a senior of indeterminate age, it had gone well and there was little to convey to the owner other than the usual post-procedure care after discharge.

"One sec," he called to the harried tech, who stopped mid-stride on his way to the kennel and turned around. "I've got an extra minute—I'll get the dog. Take five or something."

Jason knew full well that he was running late—made worse by the cat in the last appointment who hadn't been particularly cooperative with his exam. "Which kennel?"

"7B," the tech said. He smiled thankfully, dashed out the back door into the sunshine, and immediately pulled out his cell.

Curled up in 7B was a mangy, ancient, shaking mongrel, complete with a new, shiny white smile and teeth so crooked, the poor little guy was slobbering all over the floor.

"Hey, little buddy. Ready to go home?"

The dog wiggled his bottom and waddled over to the door to the crate. As soon as Jason opened it, he sprinted across the room, faster than Jason thought possible.

Fortunately, he'd closed the door to the hallway behind him.

"Trying to escape?" Jason teased as he secured a leash on the dog's collar. Once on the leash, the little dog plodded along happily next to him.

Stopping at the computer he'd abandoned in the hallway, Jason bent his head toward the screen and read the open file more carefully.

Emily Driscoll
Snaggletooth, Mixed Breed
Routine dental cleaning

Jason tamped down the rush of emotions threatening to drown him like a relentless tide.

Emily.

Whenever he saw that name, his chest tightened. It didn't matter if it was his Em or not.

It wasn't *his* Em, he told himself. *His* Em was Emily Lanson. At least it was Emily Lanson the last time he'd—

He didn't want to think about the last time he'd seen her.

Thankfully, he managed to guide the computer down the hall carefully enough to avoid being trampled by techs in full panic mode, and as a bonus, he arrived at Exam Room Two without tipping over the cart or tangling the leash in the wheels.

He pushed the door open.

And blinked.

Em—*his* Em—was standing in the room, her eyes focused on Snaggletooth in obvious relief. For a moment, he let himself gaze at her, drink her in. Her brown hair was longer than when he'd seen her last. She was thinner, too. Her cheekbones were pink from recent sunshine, and she was wearing the same perfume she always had.

His stomach lurched.

Oh no—

At the sight of her, the little dog at his feet smiled as his tail wagged violently, moving his entire backside.

"Snaggles!" she said, eyes only for the dog.

"Em—" he breathed.

At his voice, she looked up, eyes wide.

For a moment, both were frozen.

A million thoughts competed for attention at once.

The woman who was very nearly my wife.

Em stumbled backward until the back of her knees collided with a plastic chair. "What are you doing here?" she blurted.

"I—uh—am—uh—filling in…"

"No…no…no…" she said, bent down, picked up Snaggletooth, and fled out the door, his leash trailing behind them, forgotten.

SEVEN

Snaggles parked himself on the passenger seat of the Beetle and flicked his eyes back from the window periodically to glance at Emily as they sped through town, his ears flattened in distress. The tiny old dog seemed to understand the depth of her anguish.

Somehow, through wrenching sobs, she made it back to her townhouse.

Hands shaking, Emily unlocked the gate and the front door, finally collapsing on the couch inside. Warm tears dripped down her face as she dialed Jess.

"He...he..." It was all Emily could manage.

"Em? Who? What's wrong? What's happened?"

She couldn't speak.

"Em? Are you there?"

A deep breath. "Jess, he's...he's here."

"Charles is at your townhouse? What's Charles doing here?"

"No." She swallowed, gathered her courage, and for the first time in years, spoke his name aloud. "Jace."

"Jason is here? As in, *here*? In Westshore Beach?"

"Yeah."

"Shit," Jess muttered.

"You…you didn't know he lived here, did you?"

"I didn't, Em." Silence. "I'm so sorry."

"Yeah." Emily let Snaggles out into the tiny, fenced front yard and leaned on the kitchen counter, her head in her hands.

"I'll be right over," her best friend said and hung up.

Jess arrived seventeen minutes later, scrunchie trapping most of her curls in an impromptu bun on top of her head, a bottle of red wine—previously opened but nearly full—in her hand. By then, Emily's tears had stopped, replaced by an echoing numbness.

"What the hell, Em?" she asked, plunking the bottle down on the kitchen counter and prying the cork out. She rooted around on the cabinet's top shelf for two glasses.

"Exactly," Jess said.

"What's he doing here?"

"He was at the clinic when I picked up Snaggles." Tears threatened again. Emily tamped down on them, hard. She wasn't going to cry anymore. Not because of one Jason Asshole-of-the-Century Williams.

"That bastard," Jess muttered. "Like, sitting in the waiting room with a dog? I hope Snaggles bit him. What did you do?"

"He wasn't *at* the clinic. He was working as a vet there."

"What?" Jess poured a hefty glass and held it out for Emily. Red wine tended to give her a headache, but she wasn't about to say no to a glass right then.

"I called the clinic after I talked to you. Apparently, he's not part of the permanent staff there—he was filling in for another vet that had been called out of town."

"That's shit luck."

"Yeah. It is." Emily walked to the kitchen window and

looked out, watching Snaggles sniffing around at the far edge of the cedar fence.

"My mom warned me. She showed me an advertisement she got in the mail for Williams Veterinary Clinic, listing 'Jason Williams' as the vet's name. She said she wanted to prepare me in case I got a postcard in the mail myself. But you know how common 'Williams' is. I thought it was a coincidence," Emily said.

"Because he isn't a vet," Jess said.

"He wasn't the last time I saw him," Emily said. "He was in technology, like me."

"So, he became a vet sometime in the last few years and moved to Westshore? That's flipping bizarro-world."

"It's been eight years, Jess. Plenty of time to get a different degree and start your own practice." Emily laughed bitterly. "I didn't even go to the clinic on mom's postcard. I went to Beach County Animal Hospital."

"Damn," Jess said. "How could he possibly think it would be okay to move here? I mean, like, this is your hometown, not his."

"There doesn't seem to be a law that prevents lying-ass exes from moving to your favorite place in the world," Emily said.

"Sounds like we need one."

Emily took a shaky breath. "I wanted to start over after the divorce. I sold the house and had all my stuff moved. I just rented this townhouse…" A sob threatened to escape. She bit her lip to stop it.

Jess plopped down next to her and pulled her into a hug. "I know you. You can do this. You can. Don't let son-of-bitch run you off."

"I mean, I knew I would bump into Tyler at some point. Makes sense, right? He lives here. But Jace…"

"Westshore is way bigger than when you and I were in high school. I'll bet you can avoid him without too much effort. Take Snaggles to a vet a billion miles from here. Or I can take him for you."

"Maybe."

Jess got up and strode into the kitchen. "I'm sorry, Em," she said from behind the refrigerator door. "It sucks."

"It does."

"Listen," Jess said, peering around the door with a wry smile. "I know people. I can make a few calls. There are a handful of parents on the PTA that I could send over to his place. They'd show up with megaphones and demand he stay away from you. If he doesn't, they'll force him to buy an entire truckload of butter braids and organize next spring's bake sale. They'd scare him so badly he'll never step near you again."

Emily huffed a halfhearted laugh, took a deep swallow of wine, and did her best not to gag. "Good grief. I've had cough syrup that tastes better than this red. Just how cheap is this stuff?"

"Hey, not everyone can afford that Scotch you like so much. I'm a schoolteacher, remember? Plus, it makes me drunk."

"Everything makes you drunk, Jess."

"Maybe." Jess's eyes lit up. "I'll tell you what you need. You need another night on the town. Another night and I promise you'll forget all about this. Why don't you call Mike? He was interested. Seemed more than interested, to be honest. He walked all the way over to our table just to give you his number when he could have any woman in the entire place."

"I don't know."

Jess poked at a half-empty takeout box on the counter.

"You have barely been outside since you got here, and Westshore is not the kind of place where people stay inside. You lose your tan lines and the whole town starts talking. You'd probably end up on Channel 7 News, right after the weather forecast."

Emily drew her knees to her chest and wrapped her arms around them.

"It doesn't have to mean anything," Jess continued. "Go out and have fun with a cute volleyball guy. Get your mind off things. Have a couple drinks and come home."

"I'm not sure."

"You said it yourself the other day—it's not going to be easy at first. It's not easy for any of us, to be honest. But you can't win if you don't play."

"I'm making great headway on the boxes. I unpacked the dishes last night."

"The heck with the boxes. Have some fun." Jessie plunked down across from her on the carpet. "Didn't you move back to Westshore for a fresh start? Screw the boring stuff. Rather, screw the fun guy and forget about the boring stuff. And then you'll forget about lying-ass exes, too." She smiled brightly. "I'll let you borrow my yellow dress."

"Okay. Fun. Right." Emily sighed, grabbed her phone, and pulled up Mike in her contact list.

Hey Mike, it's Emily. Would you like to meet for a drink?

Barely a minute passed before her cell lit up.

7pm tonight at Gulf and Main

"Wow, that didn't take long," Jess said.

"Tonight? I can't go *tonight*."

"Sure, you can. Impetuous, right? Fun-loving? New life?"

"Spontaneous, not impetuous," Emily said.

"Right. Spontaneous."

Snaggles waddled up to the sliding glass door to be let inside.

Emily opened the door and the little dog wandered in and plopped down on his bed. "Snaggles is still really groggy. I don't want to leave him alone after all the dental work he had. If I leave, he'll think I'm going to abandon him again."

"I'll stay here and watch Snaggles," Jess offered.

"My mom needs her car tonight," Emily said. "Goat yoga or something."

"Take mine."

Her best friend was relentless.

"Okay," Emily said reluctantly.

"And I'm happy to make myself scarce if, you know, you want to give Mike a grand tour of the townhouse when you get back," Jess said with a wicked smile. "Maybe you can show him the view from your bedroom window."

"Jess, the last time I brought someone home on a first date, he wound up ripping out my heart and basically ruining my life," Emily said. "I can promise you one thing. I'm not bringing anyone here. Not now. Not ever."

Jason didn't care if stepping outside for a moment jeopardized his reciprocity agreement with Beach County Animal Hospital. He needed a minute to collect himself. Anyone would, he reasoned, if they'd just seen the woman who—

Shit.

Squinting at the late morning sun, Jason slid out the back

door of the clinic, nodded at the vet tech shouldering his way inside, and dropped down onto the sidewalk curb. His thoughts reeled.

That had been an unmitigated disaster.

Dammit, he *knew* he might bump into Em around town. She visited her mom and best friend like clockwork every second week in April and third week of December. At first, he sequestered himself at home during those times every year like a hermit, leaving the condo only to go back and forth to the clinic.

Lately, Westshore had grown big enough to avoid his ex-fiancé during those sporadic visits, and besides, Jason would be at his clinic during the day, and he didn't go out in the evenings all that much. If he knew Em—and dammit, he *did*—when she was on vacation, she'd be at the beach all day with Jessie and out for drinks in the evenings. If, by some weird chance, he saw her in the local Publix, he'd promised himself he'd make himself scarce until she was gone.

But it wasn't April or December. That either meant Em was veering out of her customary routine, which he doubted, or something else was up. She'd had a dog and an address and—

Shit. Did she live here now?

Although…the Em he knew couldn't live in Westshore permanently.

Gifted in math and science, Em had gone to college for computer programming and started her career as a developer. Within three years, she'd been promoted to a manager.

Which was when they'd met.

Driven, intelligent, and ambitious. That was his Em.

But there weren't any high-tech or consulting firms in Westshore Beach, and few jobs for information technology managers or directors. Hotels, banks, car dealerships, and restaurants, and anything feeding the tourist industry—like retail or boat rentals—were all plentiful. For Em to live here, she would have had to change her career.

Just like he did.

Damn.

Jason dragged his fingers through his hair and let his head hang down.

Why had he decided to settle in Westshore? Why was he trying to make a life here, of all places?

Truthfully? Once he realized he'd made the biggest mistake of his life, he'd decided to get as close to her memory as he could.

And that meant living here. In Westshore Beach.

His self-imposed torture.

It was twisted, and he damn well knew it.

What the hell had he been thinking?

Should he leave Westshore Beach? Disappear? Close up his practice and go somewhere completely new and start ov—

"Doctor Williams?"

He turned around to find a confused vet tech sticking his head out the door.

"I'll be right in," Jason said.

When he'd decided to move here and open his own veterinary practice, everything had seemed so simple. If, as he suspected, Em had relocated here too, things were not going to be so simple anymore.

EIGHT

Emily had arrived at Gulf and Main ridiculously early for her date with Mike. The truth was, she'd texted Mike before she'd thought the whole stupid thing through, and now that she was sitting in the booth, nursing a glass of ice water that had long ago warmed to room temperature, she'd convinced herself she'd made one colossal, ginormous, cosmic mistake.

Was she that desperate to meet someone?

No. A hundred times, no.

She knew this date with Mike was a pitiful attempt to distract herself from the pain of seeing the man who ripped her heart out of her chest with a dull, rusty knife. Yes, life had gone on without him, but his betrayal stained her skin and colored every decision she ever made with indelible ink.

Was she this desperate to distract herself from the feeling that her entire world was going to implode? That every choice she'd made so confidently was now in doubt?

Probably.

Okay, *absolutely.*

She took another sip of tepid water.

She had a date tonight. She could do this. She *could.*

Gulf and Main's door swung open to the setting sun and sweltering heat outside, and Mike sauntered in, wearing perfect jeans, perfect leather flip flops, and a perfect button-down, with rolled-up sleeves exposing swoon-worthy, perfect forearms.

He might have turned a couple of heads as he walked by. Maybe all of them.

"Hey," Mike said with a suggestion of a smile, settling in the chair across from Emily.

A petite woman with platinum blonde hair magically appeared at their table, a pristine white bar towel flung over her left shoulder. "What are you having?" she asked with the hint of a smile while placing a second ice water on the table. "Half price margaritas and apps tonight 'til six."

"I'll have a Bud. Bottle's fine, Cass," Mike responded without taking his eyes off the woman's chest.

"Do you have Lagavulin?" Emily asked.

"I don't. That's a pretty nice bottle of Scotch. Best I've got would be Johnny Walker Red."

"I'll have the house margarita," Emily said.

The bartender disappeared behind the bar.

"Scotch, huh?" Mike asked.

"It's about the only thing I like to drink."

"Well," he said, seemingly at a loss. He glanced around the bar casually, in that accessing way of his.

"What do you do for a living, Mike?" Emily asked, trying to revive the conversation.

"Financial planner," he said, turning to her with a wink. "I help people invest money to prepare for their future. There's nothing like it. Great profession for Westshore."

"I'll bet," she said.

"What have you been up to since you got back in town?" he asked.

Emily shrugged. Unpacking wasn't all that interesting, and not something she wanted to discuss anyway. "I got a dog."

Wow, so exciting. You really know how to engage in riveting conversation. Either he's going to run away screaming or die of boredom. Maybe to liven things up, he'll slip the bartender his phone number when she comes back with our drinks.

Mike raised an eyebrow.

"His name is Snaggletooth."

He laughed. "Really?"

"Yeah. He was the oldest dog the shelter had, and he'd been there the longest. I felt like he needed a friend."

"A charity case, huh? Why was he there so long?"

"He's, well, his name suits him. He's got crooked teeth in his bottom jaw, so he drools a little bit. He's very sweet, though."

Mike pulled a face. "Drools?"

"It's not as bad as it sounds." Why was she defending her choice in dogs? "Do you have any pets?"

Emily could see Mike's smirk before he lifted his glass and took another swallow of water. "Nah. Not for me."

Just like Charles. Not that I should be comparing them.

"My ex never wanted a dog, and I always did, so I thought…"

Stop babbling and get a grip. Mike doesn't want to hear about my ex-husband and whether or not he likes dogs.

Okay, she was rusty at this dating thing. She needed to figure out how to make small talk. Adults make small talk all the time. And, at least according to her mom, she was an adult. So, not that hard, right?

Pulling up a photo of Snaggles on her cell to show Mike, Emily said, "Here he is," her words sounding lame even to her own ears. She started to hand her cell to Mike, but he was staring at the bartender striding toward them with their drinks.

Emily watched Mike's gaze catch on the bartender's cleavage as she delivered the beer and the margarita and then said, "Thanks, Cass."

"You've got it," the bartender—apparently Cass—said.

She turned to Emily. "Is that your dog?" she asked. "Can I see?"

Emily handed her cell to the woman.

"Oh, my goodness, he's adorable," she said with a smile that lit up her entire face. "Looks like quite a sweetie. You know, I almost lost my dog last week to bloat. An incredible vet saved his life. Even gave me his cell number if anything comes up."

"I'm glad your dog is okay," Emily said.

"If you need a recommendation for a vet, let me know."

Emily suppressed a shudder. "I will."

Mike dismissed the bartender with a sniff and turned to Emily. "Hungry? Want to order some appetizers?"

"Sure. I'm vegan, so it can be tricky to find something on a typical pub menu."

"A vegan, huh? I didn't peg you for a tree-hugger," he said, "but whatever."

A tree-hugger? Was that a dismissal? An accusation? What was Mike trying to insinuate?

After perusing the trifold menu parked in the center of the table for a nanosecond, he waved Cass back over.

"How about some nachos?"

"Loaded?" Cass asked.

"Absolutely." He turned to Emily, leaning back in his chair and taking a long swallow of beer. "I figure you can just pick off whatever toppings you don't want."

Emily tried not to roll her eyes. It was going to be a long evening.

Jason wasn't completely sure what made him agree to have a drink with Callie and Mel. Maybe if they discovered that he was just as boring outside the clinic as inside, they'd stop hounding him to go out. Fighting the crowd for the bartender's attention at a Westshore pub had never been high on his list of exciting things to do on a Friday night. He'd rather stay at home, a tumbler filled with his favorite alcohol in one hand and a good book in the other.

Truthfully, it might be a bad idea to have drinks with the people who worked for him, but Jason wasn't exactly sure. But after bumping into Em earlier, he was confused, lonely, and, quite frankly, needed a friendly smile or two for company to boost his spirits.

As luck would have it, Mel canceled at the last minute, texting to let him know she wasn't going to be able to make it, but that Callie was on her way. Of course, Jason knew he wouldn't hear the end of it if he canceled on Callie, too.

So, here he was, sitting at Gulf and Main, waiting in the parking lot in his Jeep like some loser, waiting for his vet tech to show.

Would it be awkward now that Callie was coming by herself?

A moment later, Callie's Honda pulled into the parking lot. Jason got out of his car, crossed his arms, and leaned back on his car's hood while Callie put the finishing touches on her lipstick in her rear-view mirror.

"Hey, Doctor Williams," she said as she slid out of her seat and locked her car with a *chirp*.

"If I threaten to go home right now if you keep calling me that, will you stop?"

She giggled. "Ok, Jason," she said.

"Are you sure that Ben is okay with us being here?" he asked as he held Gulf and Main's front door open for her.

"He's completely cool with it, I promise. He knows how much I like to go out and it's not like he's anywhere nearby so he can take me out personally. Plus, I told him all about you and your awkwardly lonely life."

"I really appreciate that," he said, letting a hint of sarcasm color his words.

"Seriously, Jason, you need to get out more. Find somebody. A handsome man like you, successful, smart, kind, and compassionate. There are people out there that need you."

"I'm going to have you write my Tinder profile," he said.

"That I can do," she said.

They settled at a high table near the bar and Callie leaned over to whisper in his ear. "Isn't that bartender the owner of the rottie that had the GDV? I think her name is Cassidy. She keeps glancing over here. She's cute." Callie lifted an eyebrow and winked. "I don't know if anyone has told you, but I'm a great matchmaker."

Jason felt his face heat. "She probably recognizes me and can't place me outside the clinic. Happens all the time. Besides, she's not my type."

"Just what is your type?"

He chuckled. "We're not going there."

"How am I going to write your Tinder profile if you won't tell me your type?"

As Jason glanced around the bar looking for his preferred brand of alcohol, Callie occupied herself with the menu.

"I'm sorry that took a minute. We're short on help tonight," the bartender said as she walked up to their table. She turned to Jason with recognition in her eyes. "Hey, Doctor Williams. Fancy seeing you here."

"How's Bear doing today?" Jason asked.

"Still great. I'll never be able to thank you enough."

"It was no problem. I'm glad he did well with the surgery."

"As am I. I don't know what I'd do without that guy," she said. "So, what will it be?"

Jason motioned for Callie to order first.

"A glass of chardonnay for me," Callie said.

His glance around the bar a moment ago suggested Gulf and Main didn't carry his favorite Scotch, but he thought he would try. "Do you have Lagavulin?"

Cassidy gave him a strange look. "Afraid not. I've got Johnny Walker Red. Will that work?"

Jason tried not to grimace and ordered a beer with a barely managed smile.

"You mentioned that you were short on help. Are you looking for bartenders?" Callie asked.

"Maybe. Know someone?"

"I bartended while I was in college," Callie said. "If you're looking, I'm interested."

"Stop by tomorrow around four and we'll talk," Cassidy said and vanished to get their drinks.

"I never know what you're going to say," Jason said with a chuckle.

"I could use something to do to keep me occupied in the evenings. And I could use the extra money since I'm only part-time at the clinic. Not to mention that this would be a great place to further hone my matchmaking skills."

"I thought you already were a master matchmaker."

"I am, but there's always room for growth. Besides, I like to share my skills with the universe. You know, poor lonely souls in need."

"Like me," Jason said with a wry smile.

"Yup. Like you."

A moment later, Callie excused herself to the restroom and Cassidy returned with the beer and wine.

"Would you run a tab for us?" Jason asked.

"Not a chance. These are on the house, as are all the drinks you will ever order in my place." Cassidy paused. "So funny. I've owned this bar for seven years. No one has ever asked me for Lagavulin until tonight. And now two people have within the last hour."

As Cassidy returned to the bar, Jason saw her glance toward a table in the corner.

He looked over to where she'd glanced—and felt his heart sink. His Em was sitting at the corner table with a giant of a guy. She was sitting with her back to them, brown hair cascading down her back like a waterfall.

He knew that hair smelled like fresh roses.

He knew it felt like silk when it slipped between his fingers.

He remembered how she liked it when he—*dammit.*

While he watched, Em said something to her date, and stood up abruptly, abandoning her unfinished drink. Em's face flushed. The guy pounded his beer and stalked out, looking disgruntled. Was it a boyfriend? A husband? When he saw her at the clinic, he hadn't had time to notice if she were wearing a ring, but she'd listed a different last name on Snaggle's file.

Shit.

Callie returned from the bathroom and sat down. "What's wrong? You look like you've seen a ghost."

He cleared his throat. "I think I might have."

"Upon further reflection, the bartender is not for you," Callie said as she picked up her glass and swirled the wine in the light. "But I met someone in the restroom who I think is perfect for you. She's sitting over there—"

Callie turned toward the table Em and her date had just deserted. "But it looks like she's gone."

NINE

The nachos had arrived in all their glory.

The server gave Mike a fleeting, sidelong glance and darted away too quickly for Emily to politely inquire how many different dead animals had been absorbed into the otherwise innocent chips. Even the once wholesome beans, no doubt, contained lard.

Pig butt fat, her brain corrected. *No need to waddle around the truth.*

The refried bean's questionable contents didn't matter, anyway. Beef and cheese smothered every tortilla chip, and simply glancing at the plate dripping with grease robbed her of any interest in food. In fact, if she kept looking at the soggy limpness masquerading as an appetizer, the current, lonely contents of her stomach might make an appearance themselves.

Mike dove in with a single-minded frenzy. The table tilted. Chips flew. Did he realize she was still there?

Warning. Turbulence. Remain in your vehicle and keep your arms inside at all times.

Jace had always—

Dammit. Why, *why* was she thinking of Jace while she was on a date with a six-foot-two, drop-dead gorgeous specimen who could dazzle the pants off anyone in this bar with a mere flex of his bicep?

If anything, I should be thinking of Charles, right? Wouldn't comparing Mike to my newly minted ex-husband be reasonable at least?

It was as if her brain completely forgot she was married for four entire *years* after the disaster with Jace in Mexico. As if there was a gap in her memory where Jace had seeped in like fungus.

Frustrated, Emily glanced around.

Honestly, The Pub at Gulf and Main was a cute little place. Laidback. Local. Comfortable.

Across the room, a woman in a staggeringly pink dress chatted animatedly with her date. Emily couldn't quite see the man's face from the table where she was sitting. The woman swirled her glass of ice water, beaming at something her date said.

People were happy here. Maybe she could be one of those people.

"Emily?"

Dammit, she'd drifted off again. What had Mike been saying?

"Will you excuse me?" Emily said.

Picking up her purse, she made her way down the hall to the restroom. While Emily was fixing her lipstick, the woman in the blinding pink minidress pushed open the door. She flashed Emily a warm smile and vanished into one of the stalls, humming.

Emily glanced in the mirror again and frowned. Her gray outfit was the color of the numbingly cold clouds of a Virginia winter. She lived at the beach now and it was *summer.* Drab gray was probably as illegal in Westshore as tan lines.

She'd have to convince Jess to go shopping with her later this week.

When she returned to the table, Mike glanced at the spongy remains of cheese bonded to the plate in front of him and said, "You missed out. They were great."

"Maybe Gordon Ramsey is assisting in the kitchen," Emily said.

He shrugged.

"I haven't heard any swearing, or yelling, or swearing *with* yelling, so probably not," she added.

Mike grunted.

A server breezed by to collect the empty plate.

"They were awful," Mike quipped. "Hated them. Nearly called the manager. You guys need to do something about those nachos."

The server rolled her eyes. Emily pinched her lips together to keep herself from laughing.

"So…" he said.

"So…" she said.

Two minutes of silence later, she'd had enough. "You know, Mike, I was up late last night unpacking so I'm getting kind of tired. Would it be ok if we called it a night?"

He seemed to want to say something and then changed his mind. "Sure," he said with a half-hearted smile.

Grabbing her purse, Emily rose from the table. As she stood, she was able to see what she couldn't while she was seated—the pretty woman from the bathroom's date.

She would know that face anywhere.

Jace.

She felt her face flush as her stomach sank with the weight of the Titanic.

Just like our relationship. Somewhere at the bottom of the Atlantic. Or, in this case, the Gulf of Mexico.

Emily took a step and stumbled.

"Hey there, little lady. That was only one drink. Bit of a lightweight, huh?" Mike said with a chuckle, taking her arm. "I can give you a ride if you want."

"It was just my shoe getting caught on the edge of the chair." She managed a smile through clenched teeth and kept her gaze away from Jace and his date? His girlfriend? His...*wife*? "Thanks, though."

"Maybe we can do this again?" Mike asked. "We can finish up another night."

"Uh, sure."

"I'll shoot you a text."

Mike's gaze parked on her lips, and Emily fought the urge to run.

"Okay," and she spun toward the door, too overwhelmed to do anything but dart to the safety of her best friend's battered Toyota.

For the second time in a single day, Emily wasn't sure how she managed to drive home.

"You're back early. So, how'd it go?" Jess called from the living room as Emily shut the front door of the townhouse behind her.

Emily flopped down on the couch next to her best friend, tossing her cell and Jess's keys on the coffee table. A sleepy Snaggles wandered over and plunked down at her feet. "Jace was there."

"Wait. Wait. *Jace* was on your date?"

"No. He was at Gulf and Main. With someone."

"Well, shit."

"Yeah."

"Well, double shit," Jess elaborated.

"You said that," Emily said. "Mostly."

"I'm just beating a dead horse to death," Jess clarified.

Groaning, Emily let herself fall back into the cushions. Maybe she could hide out in between the couch's fluffiness until…well, until forever. No one would even notice she was gone. Right?

"I haven't seen him in eight years and now he's everywhere!" Emily said, her voice muffled by the pillows.

"I'm sorry, hon. It bites." Jess rose to take her empty wine glass into the kitchen. "But how'd it go with Mike?"

"Ugh."

"You've barely given it a chance," Jess called. The fridge door squeaked. "You weren't even there an hour."

"You're right. I couldn't stay after seeing Jace there."

Maybe closing her eyes would help? Or a fuzzy blanket? Yes, a blanket would be nice.

She felt Jess sit back down next to her. A bag rustled nearby.

"Tortilla chips? I brought salsa, too. I could make them into nachos."

Emily groaned loud enough to startle Snaggles.

Her cell phone vibrated. Jess picked it up, muttered a black curse under her breath, and handed it to Emily.

Hey. It's Jace. Saw you at Gulf and Main. Wondering if we can talk?

"How did he even get your number?" Jess asked.

"I never changed it. Or he could have gotten it off Snaggle's records."

Emily typed the first response she could think of.

you're about eight years too late for that

"I bet he could get disbarred for that," Jess said. "Those are confidential animal patient records. They're not for nosing through to find your ex's number who doesn't want anything to do with you."

"He's not a lawyer, Jess. He's a vet. They don't get disbarred."

"Vets must have something like that." Jess started furiously typing on her cell. "See?" she said, tilting the screen toward Emily. "They can lose their license."

Emily sighed.

"You need to block his sorry ass," Jess said.

"He's never shied away from difficult conversations," Emily argued.

"Did you hear what you just said? I mean, Em, come on. He ghosted you in the worst way possible, like some kind of sick freak." Jess sighed. "So, are you going to meet him or block him?"

"It doesn't have to be one or the other."

"I think maybe it does," Jess said.

Emily rolled her eyes and retreated deeper into the pillows.

TEN

It had been a hell of a couple of days.

After noticing Em on a date at Gulf and Main, he'd done his best to keep up the conversation with Callie but truthfully, he'd failed epically.

When was the last time I handled anything outside my veterinary practice well? Shit, I probably owe Callie an apology for completely checking out.

Callie was sweet, open, and engaging—just the sort of woman he wanted to fall in love with. Except every time he'd convinced himself to go on a date since walking away from Em—not that there had been many dates between veterinary school and setting up his new practice—something was missing. Something tangible, something necessary.

No, not some*thing*. Some*one*.

That someone was Em.

And Jason had blown any chance he had of a future with her eight long years ago.

Now, he couldn't go anywhere in Westshore Beach without bumping into her. First the clinic, now the pub.

And the look on her face when he'd walked into the exam

room?

Maybe it was simple surprise. Maybe he'd just caught her off guard. But maybe, just maybe, it was anger. Or hurt. And anger or hurt might mean Em still cared.

That was a veritable truckload of *maybes*.

He was thinking in circles, and it was no use.

Leaning back deeper into the couch, Jason sighed.

What he needed was advice. And the best person to dispense that advice was currently a couple of continents away.

As soon as Tyler gets home, I'll ask him how to handle the situation with Em. He'll know.

His cousin was an expert at getting to the heart of things, cutting through the unimportant stuff, and figuring out the essence of what truly mattered. He could sit with Tyler for hours while the man downed beer after beer, asking pointed and insightful questions that had never occurred to Jason, leading him to the answers that had been right underneath the surface all along.

Tyler had been the one who set him on the path back to living after Jason made the worst mistake of his life. The person that convinced him to set up his veterinary practice in Westshore Beach. He was exactly who Jason needed, and he'd be back from Africa next week.

It couldn't come soon enough.

Saturday morning dawned bright and sunny, and by 5:30 a.m., caffeine had performed its perfect magic, and Jason was halfway to the clinic to check on the cats and dogs recovering from surgical procedures.

Other than the snide reply by text—which, admittedly, he deserved—there had been no word from Em. In the silence, he'd started to convince his heart that he'd never hear from her again.

It's okay if I never do, he repeated to himself. *I'll be okay if I never do.*

On the passenger seat, his phone vibrated.

His heart leapt.

But it wasn't a reply from Em. The text was from Tyler— back in the US early, after more than a month in Africa.

Arrived home yesterday. Grab a beer tonight?

Sounds great

Jason could almost hear Tyler's shock through his cell.

Gulf and Main 8pm

Jason groaned. Wasn't there another bar in all of Westshore Beach? His adopted hometown was about to become a minefield of: *Is that Em in checkout line six? Why is her car parked in front of Fire Station Seven? Is that her two rows back in the movie theater?*

He didn't want to avoid—

The hell with it. The possibility of bumping into Em isn't going to keep me from seeing my cousin.

Emily knocked as she pushed Jess's front door open.

"Hey!"

"Hey," Jess called back. "Come on in and make yourself at home."

Her best friend's condo was as it had always been. A haphazard pile of textbooks teetered on an end table, despite a bookshelf with ample space for more. Scattered capless red pens, discarded water bottles, random dirty coffee mugs, and various homemade teacher appreciation gifts littered the space, the detritus in danger of forming a sentient being and vocally complaining about the mess.

Emily shoved some debris aside and sunk into Jess's ridiculously comfy couch.

"Sorry about the state of things," Jess said from the kitchen—the same thing she repeated whenever Emily came over.

A large book of photography, *Capturing the Big Five* by Tyler Dawson, peeked out from amongst the chaos on the coffee table.

Tyler Dawson, world-famous wildlife photographer—and Jace's cousin and best friend. Emily studied the book's cover for a moment then picked it up, upending several pencils in the process. A lopsided macaroni rainbow, glued to blue construction paper and inscribed with *Thank You Miss Langston* in bold, red crayon, floated to the floor. She left it where it landed.

From the kitchen, Jess called, "Iced coffee?"

"Sure."

The sound of frantic washing and banging of cabinets ensued.

Emily turned the book over. A photograph of Tyler, laying on his belly in a field of tall grass, graced the back cover. Even holding a magnificent camera capped with an enormous lens, he looked like a predator himself. His dark hair—so much like Jace's—appeared as if it had been mussed into perfection by a gentle breeze. His skin, kissed by the African sun. A pair of aviators were perched on his head, his gaze focused on something outside the frame.

He was as stunning as the photographs inside.

Emily hadn't seen Tyler since Cancún. If anything, the last eight years had honed his features until they were flawless. He'd always been attractive, but now he was drop-dead, out-of-this-world gorgeous.

The description under his photograph enumerated accolades from National Geographic and more than a handful of Photographer of the Year awards. Unsurprisingly, *Capturing the Big Five* was a New York Times Bestseller.

So, Tyler had made it big. Very big.

It seemed Emily had been living under a rock.

Page after page contained breathtaking images of lions, leopards, rhinos, elephants, and what the captions identified as *Cape Buffalo* in stunning color. Each image told its own story: a family of elephants tossing mud on their backs; a lioness with a cub between her teeth; a herd of giraffes outlined by a golden sun.

Emily flipped to the front page. The dedication was simply:

> *My Jess,*
> *Ever thankful we figured it out between us.*
> *-Ty*
>
> *P.S., The blending of idioms is called a malaphor.*
> *P.P.S., Maybe take it easy on the metaphors and the idioms?*

A line in blue ink had been scrawled underneath the printed text in Tyler's sloppy hand:

> *I love you, Jess.*

Her best friend emerged from the kitchen, two

mismatched glasses of iced coffee in hand.

"Jess...?" Emily said, nodding at the open book on her lap.

"Oh. That." Her best friend plopped down next to her and handed her a glass. An orange construction paper cut-out of a hand transformed into a cross-eyed turkey drifted from the couch to the carpet. "I wasn't sure how to tell you."

"Wait. Are you and Tyler...?" Emily couldn't bring herself to ask her best friend if she was sleeping with Jace's cousin. "You two were always—I don't know—close? No, that's the wrong word. Circling each other like two cats. I never knew if you were going to tear each other into pieces or tear each other's clothes off."

Jess huffed a laugh and took a swallow of iced coffee, sighing appreciatively. "Love and hate. Same emotion, different sides of the same mirror."

"So, what's going on between you?"

"My relationship with Ty has always been complicated. But we—like he said in the dedication—figured it out."

Emily raised an eyebrow and waited.

"I'm sorry I never told you." She cleared her throat. "We sorta tried, I guess? Two—no, three years ago, now. We were both terribly drunk. Took an Uber to his house after getting completely smashed at Gulf and Main. There was a moment when I thought he might, you know, actually kiss me, but instead he just kind of backed up and laughed nervously. So, yeah. We ordered a pizza and curled up to Netflix and that was that."

"What do you mean, 'that was that'?"

A sigh. "Look. I love him. I do. And he loves me. But not like that." Jess shuddered. "Not going there again, like ever. I made my bed, and now I have to throw it out with the bathwater."

"Do you ever see him?"

Jess smiled. "Yeah. A lot. He pays me."

"He pays you to see him?"

Her best friend barked a laugh. "You should see your face. You know not to play poker, right? Because you couldn't keep what you're thinking off your face if you tried."

Emily snapped her mouth shut.

"Ty hired me to watch his place whenever he's out of the country on assignment." Jess took a careful swallow of coffee. "He lives off Old State Road 72 now. He owns ten acres and a couple of horses. I don't take care of the horses—he's got the kids that live next door doing that—they're getting credit for a 4-H project or something—but I stop by his place, get his mail, make sure it looks occupado. It's a great side gig." She smiled widely. "He'll be back today. I can't wait to see him."

"You're serious."

"As serious as taxes." Jess pursed her lips. "Are you mad that I didn't tell you?"

Emily sighed. "No. I understand why you didn't."

"I'm sorry, Em," she said. "Everything to do with...*him* is so murky. I never even know if I can say his name without bringing up all that hurt for you."

"And I appreciate that." Emily cleared her throat. "If I can say it, you can say it," she said. "His name is Jason Williams."

ELEVEN

Jess, as usual, was late.

Technically, her best friend was *almost* late. Which, as far as Emily was concerned, was *exactly* the same as being late.

Emily glanced around the pub once again. Desperately trying to save the last unoccupied barstool for Jess—if the woman ever bothered to show up before Emily died of either boredom or old age—she yanked it closer. The press of the crowd leaning in to get the bartender's attention made her wary of setting her margarita in front of the open barstool next to her. She'd ask the bartender for an extra glass of water to place there if she could ever catch the poor harried woman's eye.

She recognized the bartender from her first date with Mike—the woman who asked about Snaggle's picture and said that she could recommend a good vet in Westshore. Before Emily could fully form that thought—

"Is this seat taken?"

Emily nodded, certain the guy couldn't hear her above the din. He was tall, deeply tan, and wearing a baseball cap. The scraggly beginnings of a beard dusted his jaw. He smiled a thank you and backed away a half-step to wait for his beer.

She glanced at her phone, hoping to avoid conversation.

In three and a half minutes, Jess would technically be late.

Eventually, Baseball-Cap-Guy received his bottle of Bud and someone else slid into the open space.

"House margarita," he said, in a voice she'd recognize anywhere.

Her heart caught in her throat.

Jace.

After ordering, Jace took a step back from the stool and waited with his hands in his pockets.

A breath later, he noticed her.

He seemed to be caught between saying hello and offering her a small smile.

Emily glanced around. *Where the hell is Jess?*

The front door opened, and Mike sauntered in. Certain Mike would insist on sitting next to her until Jess arrived, she turned to Jace. "I'm saving that seat for Jess. I hate to ask you a favor, but it'd be great if you could keep it occupied until she arrives."

He nodded. "Tyler is supposed to meet me here. I promise once he arrives, I'll move," her ex-fiancé replied evenly.

The bartender placed a margarita in front of Jace and said, "Hey now, is that any kind of promise a nice guy like you should be making?" She turned to Emily. "This is exactly who you want sitting next to you." The bartender paused putting glasses away and leaned on the bar toward them. "He's a hero."

Shaking his head, Jace slid into the stool next to Em and laid his phone on the bar. "Calling me a hero is a bit much, Cass. I was just doing my job."

Cass ignored him. "Best vet in town. Saved my dog a

couple of weeks back."

"You mentioned that when I was here last time," Emily said. "Is he paying you for advertising?"

"Nope." The bartender huffed a laugh. "So, you two know each other?"

Emily didn't look in Jace's direction. "You could say that."

Nodding, Cass turned away to fill more orders. Emily studied her drink.

Dammit all to hell, she could *smell* him. Him and his stupid cologne. What had made her ask him to sit down? Oh, yeah, having to deal with Mike and his vapid conversation skills. Caught between a proverbial rock and a hard place.

So to speak.

Jace's phone lit up.

Emily couldn't help but notice his smile as he read the text. "Good news?" she asked snidely.

"Not exactly." He shrugged. "Remember Colleen Barshaw?"

Emily laughed bitterly. "Yup."

"She's married now. Lives in Connecticut. Two kids."

Emily managed an inarticulate response then pursed her lips.

"We keep in touch," Jace continued as if it were the most reasonable thing on earth to say. "Check-in and say hello every once in a while."

"Right." Emily took a sip of her margarita and narrowed her eyes. "And how does her husband feel about that?"

"I'll ask him next time I see him. We're supposed to meet in Rocky Mountain National Park for a hiking trip in October."

Emily suppressed the need to roll her eyes. This was the man she knew, with his never-ending perfect excuses, perfect reasons.

Perfect lies.

They sat in silence for a moment while Emily finished her margarita.

"Can I get you another?" Jason asked.

"Why not?"

Jace waved, and a different bartender sped over, smiling at him—the blonde woman in the pink dress that had been on a date with him. The same woman Emily had spoken to in the bathroom. Today, she was wearing a lime green t-shirt with a deep V-neck, cut-off shorts, and plastic neon yellow earrings in the shape of palm trees.

Her smile was a bright as her earrings. Wiping her hands on a bar towel, she said, "Hey, Boss."

"Hey yourself, Callie."

"Another margarita, please," he said, nodding toward Emily's empty cup.

When she disappeared, Emily said, "Let me guess. Another one of your patients at the clinic? Save her dog, too? Did she take you out for drinks to thank you?"

Jace raised an eyebrow. "Callie doesn't have a dog, but she does have two cats. Siblings, both black and white. Adorable little things."

"So, she's yet another conquest. Should I give her a heads-up about your disappearing act?"

"Em..." Jace shook his head. "She works for me part-time as a vet tech."

Emily snorted, watching the greenish liquid slosh around the ice cubes as she tipped her plastic cup.

"Do you think we could talk sometime?" he asked. "About what happened?"

She tossed the dregs of the margarita down, the sour lime making her thirsty. Narrowing her eyes, she said, "If you see

Jess, tell her I had to go."

Tossing a twenty on the bar, Emily abandoned her barstool and disappeared into the crowd before he could say anything more.

Jason blinked at the empty stool where Em had been sitting a moment before.

Well, it wasn't surprise on her face this time. Nope. That was most definitely anger.

He watched Em shove her way through the crowd pressing into the bar to order the last round before happy hour was officially over, her shoulders tight, lips pursed. He could understand her anger, but her open hostility shocked him. That wasn't the Em he remembered.

Am I the asshole that made her that way? Was what I did to her to blame?

A moment later, Tyler thumped Jason's shoulder in greeting, pulled out the stool that Em had abandoned, dropped into it, and caught Cass's attention with a jerk of his chin and one of his easy smiles.

Cass came over to take Tyler's drink order, her eyes lingering a moment too long on his cousin's face as the barest blush colored her cheekbones. Jace was used to it. Tyler was always popular with women—until he opened his mouth.

"What's going on, my brother?" Tyler asked, turning away from the bartender.

"How was your trip?" Jason asked. "Where were you again?"

"Zimbabwe this time. Near Victoria Falls, if that helps."

"Sort of."

"Got some great shots," Tyler continued. "Working with Nat Geo has been flipping amazing. You'll have to come with me one of these times. See lions and elephants for yourself."

"I know. Next year, maybe," Jason said. "After I bring on another vet for the clinic."

"Speaking of that, how's the clinic?"

"Things are good. Patients have doubled in the last two months."

"Double of a small number is still small, but that sounds like it could be a positive trend."

Jason swallowed a smile. Tyler was a good guy, just never made it easy on anyone, including him. *Especially* him. "Never one to mince words, are you, cuz?"

Tyler huffed a laugh. "But that's not what I was initially asking about. I asked what was going on."

Jason raised an eyebrow. "What do you mean, what's going on?"

"You tell me."

Tyler could be an aggravating prick, to be honest. But at least you always knew where you stood with him.

"Something's up," Tyler continued. "You never agree to meet me for drinks here."

"You gain psychic abilities in the last eight weeks?" Jason asked.

"Yeah, I stepped in a steaming pile of lion scat and now I can tell when people are bullshitting me. It's magic."

Jason let out a long breath through his nose. "Emily is in town." It felt strange to say her name aloud.

"Hmmm," Tyler said around his newly delivered beer.

"More specifically, she's moved back to town."

"Ah," Tyler said as if that explained everything.

"I ran into her at Beach County Animal Hospital while I was covering for another vet. She adopted a rescue." Jason took a long swallow of his margarita to quell the panic rising in his stomach. "I think it was fair to say we were both a bit surprised."

Tyler nodded and took another slow swallow of beer. "Still angry, I'd bet."

"Yeah."

"Cancún was a fucking disaster. You ripped her heart out. She probably wouldn't have moved to Westshore if she knew you lived here."

"Don't mince words, brother."

"You know I don't." Tyler pushed his empty beer bottle away and motioned to Cass for another. "I never will."

"I know it's my fault but, damn," Jason said, thinking of what she'd said when she'd been next to him just moments ago.

Tyler nodded his thanks at Cass as she set the next beer down in front of him, then looked Jason in the eye. "Did you try to contact Emily after seeing her at the clinic?"

"I texted her to see if she would meet me somewhere and talk."

"I'm assuming she didn't agree."

"I didn't hear back," Jason said, the lie making him queasy.

"What are you going to do about it?" Tyler asked.

"Nothing. There's not a damn thing to be done."

"Hmmm," Tyler said again.

"Okay, fine. What would you do?"

"Ask her again," Tyler said. "You have to clear the air. Let the things that need to be said, be said. Otherwise, you both will avoid each other, and this town is too fucking small for that bullshit to work out for the best."

Jason sighed. "I wouldn't even know where to start."

Tyler didn't say anything for a while, just sipped his beer. "How about apologizing for abandoning her days before you were supposed to marry her, and vanishing into thin air?"

Jason took a long swallow of his drink.

"Here's some advice," Tyler continued. "When Emily starts talking—and she will—shut up and listen. If you ever loved her, give her a chance to say what she needs to say so she can move on from her anger."

Tyler's phone buzzed, and as he looked down a small smile threatened the corners of his mouth as he typed his reply.

Thankful for the opportunity to change the subject, Jason asked, "Someone I should know about?"

"Nope," Tyler said, setting his phone face down on the bar and picking up his beer. "If you must know, it was someone I was sitting next to on the plane."

"You sure get into other people's shorts but have no tolerance for people in yours."

"There's no room in my shorts for anything other than what's already in there." He tossed Jason a cocky smile. "And in case you're wondering, I haven't heard from Emily in years. Jess doesn't mention her that often, and when she does, I think it's a slip. I think it's just too awkward for her to go there with me. But I know they're still good friends."

"How is Jessie, by the way?"

"She's good."

"When are you going to marry her?"

"Didn't I mention there wasn't any room in my shorts for you?" Tyler said, his smile becoming smug. "I love Jess, but she and I are just friends. We'll always be friends, and that's it."

TWELVE

"**H**ey. I'm here," Jess called as she pushed open Emily's front door with her shoulder, two reusable grocery bags in hand. "I brought some snacks, well, because I'm going to be here for a few hours, and you have exactly zero in the house."

"How do you know I don't have any snacks?" Emily asked.

"Well, do you?"

"Nope."

Her best friend offered a knowing smile and set the packages on the kitchen counter. "Right."

Jace's text from the week before—arriving after she'd bolted out of Gulf and Main as if rabid wolves were at her heels—had shocked her.

Please can we meet and talk, say anything you want/need to

Part of her wanted to see him. Part of her wanted to scream at him. Part of her ached to be near him.

And the rest of her? What was left hated the part of her

that ached to be near him.

Such a pleasant mix. Like listening to a symphony that used jackhammers for the percussion section.

It had taken Emily all of three hours and twenty-seven minutes to type her reply, only after convincing herself that she could change her mind later if she wanted to.

ok

She'd typed the simple word and willed her hands not to fidget while she waited for a response. It came immediately.

Meet at 16th Ave beach? Day/time?

Meet at the beach where he asked me to marry him? Has he lost his mind? Or has he forgotten everything that had to do with us?
This reply took her no time at all.

not there

After a moment of thought, she'd suggested the somewhat neutral territory of North Cove Beach in three days, hoping like hell that she hadn't lost her mind, too.

Jason had agreed, and now, three agonizingly long days later, Emily was watching her best friend unpack the snacks she'd brought—a smorgasbord of chips ending in '*-itos*': Doritos, Tostitos, Fritos.

Emily cringed.

The last seventy-two hours had awoken all the emotion that lay buried for the last eight years: the anger, the shock, the sorrow. It welled up inside her and threatened to boil over and touch everything in her brand-new life in Westshore. She needed it gone.

She glanced at the clock. In a couple minutes, she'd have to decide if she was actually going to get in her car and drive to North Cove or not.

Well, I could always pull a no-show, as petty as that would look. Give him a taste of his own medicine.

Snaggles ambled over to the kitchen, his backend rocking in time with his tail.

"Hey, buddy," Jess said, bending down to pet the little dog. "I brought something for you." She produced a squeak toy from one of the grocery bags and offered it to him. Gently, Snaggles grabbed it with his teeth and proudly brought it over to his bed.

"I leave for a few years, and you turn into a dog person," Emily said. "Who'd have thought."

"I'd totally get a dog if I were ever home," Jess said. "Maybe even a whole pack. That way, I won't end up being the crazy cat lady when I'm old and alone. I'll be the crazy *dog* lady. Huge difference. Huge."

"Who are you and what have you done with my best friend?"

Jess huffed a laugh. "You look amazing, by the way," she said. "I hope he eats his fucking heart out, that rat bastard."

"Thanks, Jess." Emily gave her what she hoped amounted to a smile.

"Let's toast before you go," Jess said, raising her glass of water. "To big girl panties and whatnot."

"To big girl panties," Emily repeated, raising her water bottle even as her stomach sank.

"Go," Jess said. "Tell the asshat all the things. I'll spend the evening raiding your wine rack for the pairing with these genuine gourmet chips, and, you know, picking up things because this place is an utter, complete pigsty," she said, glancing around at the pristine counters and perfectly stacked, broken-down cardboard boxes. She pulled Emily into a fierce, brief hug. "Snaggles and I will be waiting right here when you get back."

When Emily padded onto the sand at North Cove Beach, Jace was already sitting on the edge of a beach towel facing the sun as it crept toward where it would greet the gulf. His dark hair rustled gently in the gulf breeze, reminding her of the picture of Tyler, featured on the back of his photography book.

Emily lowered herself down onto the other side of the beach towel, making sure to keep a couple of feet between her and her ex-fiancé.

He didn't turn.

The air, heavy with salt, carried the cries of hungry gulls from the shoreline stretching north and a hint of the cologne he always wore. She followed his gaze out to the coral light fanning out over the water, where sky met deep blue.

On the other side of the Gulf of Mexico lay the beach where she and Jace were supposed to promise each other the rest of their lives.

It seemed impossibly far away.

"Say what you came to say," Jace said, his eyes on the restless tide stretching before them.

Emily stared at the waves breaking along the beach and gathered her strength. "You left me."

Her voice was stronger than she thought it would be. Clearer.

He didn't reply.

"No, that's not even close. It's more than that. Much more. You ghosted me three days before we were supposed to be married. *Three days*, Jace."

"I—" He stopped.

"Why?"

Jace bent forward to rest his elbows on his knees and let his head hang, dragging his fingers through his thick hair. A memory surfaced, how soft his hair felt in her fingers.

She shoved the memory away.

"I don't know what I was thinking. I don't have a good reason for what I did. I was scared. Absolutely terrified of getting married. But that's no excuse for what I did or how I treated you. I hurt you. I hurt everyone." He turned and met her eyes then. "I made the single worst decision of my life. I'm sorry."

She let his words drift in the air, floating until they thinned to nothing.

The gulls continued their cries.

Minutes passed.

Finally, Emily found her voice. "You were my whole world. I would have done anything for you. Anything. And you disappeared. No discussion, no message, no note, no phone call. Before I got back from Mexico, you had quit your job, changed your number, and *moved.* I mean, what the actual hell?"

Jace covered his head in his hands.

"Is that why you insisted on a tiny destination wedding, with what, a dozen people attending? And convinced me to arrive before you did and then meet you in Cancún? You planned it. You knew you weren't going to show."

"Em—"

"You never intended to marry me, did you?"

He glanced up, and she saw surprise light his eyes. "It wasn't like that."

"How could it not be?" she asked. "It's the only thing that makes sense. People don't vanish like that unless they plan it for weeks or months in advance."

He winced.

"I called the *police*, Jace. The *police*. I called hospitals. Nothing. I went to your apartment when I got back, and it was empty."

Jace sighed raggedly but didn't reply.

Anger welled from deep within her, sharp and raw. How could she have been so stupid as to fall for this man's lies?

"I happened to notice that Colleen was also a no-show. So did everyone else."

"What—"

"Colleen didn't show at the wedding either." Emily tried to keep the bitterness out of her voice and failed. "You know, your ex? The one who texted you last week at the bar? Wait," she said snidely. "I should be more specific, since they've all probably texted you within the last week. Colleen is the one that you insisted on inviting. The one that was supposed to be one of the witnesses at the ceremony. I bet you guys had a long laugh over that one."

"Her father had been hospitalized with a stroke. He was in intensive care for a week. In the confusion, she'd forgotten to call us."

Emily gritted her teeth and nodded. *Fine.*

"Do you have any idea what it was like for me when you left?" she asked.

Jace shook his head.

"I was mortified. My mom, my friends—no one knew what to say or what to do." She struggled to steady her voice. She promised herself she'd be strong. And she would be. "But do you know what was even worse than the embarrassment? I never got a chance to say goodbye. It was like you *died* unexpectedly. You did that to me. The man who supposedly loved me. *You.*"

As big as Jace was, he seemed to close in on himself, his shoulders shrinking, his brows pressed together, his knees pulled into his chest. "I can never make it up to you, Em."

"You asked me to share the rest of your life, Jace. I trusted you. I loved you. And I deserved more than that as your future wife. I deserved more than that as a human being."

"You're right," he said quietly.

Lips pursed, Emily blew a long breath out of her nose. "Why in the hell did you move here?"

Jace turned his gaze toward the setting sun, partially obscured by a cloud as its tip kissed the horizon. "It's hard to explain."

"I suggest that you try."

He nodded. "After I finished a six-month contract in a clinic near Gainesville, I wanted to open my own practice. I drove down to visit Tyler and looked into the veterinary clinics here. The demographics suggested that Westshore could support another one. Maybe two."

"Demographics? Seriously? You moved here because the statistics suggested Westshore could support another vet? This is *my* hometown. Didn't you think that you might bump into, oh, I don't know, my *mom* in Starbucks? Or maybe my best friend?"

"You knew I always liked Westshore," Jace said.

"I did. But you and I could never move here. No high-tech jobs for either of us." She realized she'd said *us*. *Dammit.*

Forcing herself to continue, she said, "And there must be plenty of communities that need more vets, so that's not the whole story."

Jace seemed to resign himself to sharing his next words. "When I realized what I did and how badly I messed up, I wanted you back. I figured you wouldn't take me back. I mean, I ruined everything." His jaw clenched as if he were steeling himself to admit something. "It was selfish for me to move to Westshore, I know. But it had been years since we were…" He swallowed. "I figured you'd moved on. I knew you'd visit your mom and Jessie occasionally. You'd show up with a husband and seeing me wouldn't even matter. If I could see that you were happy—just a glimpse—I'd—"

"You'd feel less guilt about what you did?"

He scooped up a handful of shells and pushed them around his palm, letting the grains of sand fall through his fingers. "Living here has been part comfort, part torture, Em. Maybe I chose it because I needed to somehow pay for how much I hurt you, by hurting myself."

"That is seriously messed up."

"I suppose it is," he conceded. Jace glanced at her left hand, where she'd worn Charles's ring for the last four years. She'd replaced it with a simple band she'd bought herself. "You married."

A guess. A correct one.

"I did."

"I'm glad."

Emily huffed a bitter laugh. "I'm not married anymore."

"Oh," he said. "I'm sorry."

"It's fine."

"Is it?"

"Is anything?"

Her question hung in the air until the sound of waves dragged it back into the gulf.

"What do you want, Em? What can I do?"

"I'm not sure. But I am sure of one thing. We won't ever be friends."

"I'm sorry to hear that," he said.

"I bet you are," she said. "Because you have every ex-girlfriend programmed into your speed dial, right? Just like Colleen has yours?"

"Em—"

"I know what you do—you pester your exes until you get past the awkwardness of your breakup, until you're convinced your friendship with them is intact. It's a lame attempt to make up for breaking up with them because of your truckload of commitment issues. Ease the hurt with undying, super supportive friendship because magically makes all the past go away." Emily turned to sneer at him. "It's ridiculous."

His eyebrows rose.

"I know why you agreed to meet me here—you're going to try to convince me that we can be friends. Guess what? You and I will *never* be friends. I don't want you in my life. I don't want to hear from you. I don't want calls or texts from you. I refuse to listen to you describe having drinks with your next girlfriend and cheering you on and sending you encouraging texts and virtual high-fives as you respond to DMs on your dating app. No. Thanks."

Jace opened his mouth to speak, but nothing came out.

"You get to suffer my ire for the rest of your life."

"Em—"

"Let me make sure you understand so it's crystal clear. We aren't friends. We will never be friends," she said.

"I—"

"I don't care what you think of me. My feelings on this don't make me a monster," Emily added. "They make me human."

Jace took a moment to respond. "You were never fully comfortable with my friendships," he said. "But I never cheated on you, Em. Never. I might be friends with every woman I've ever dated—except for you—but I never once stepped out on you."

"If you're suggesting I take any responsibility for what you did to me—to us—you're insane. Just because I didn't like your exes having so much influence over your life doesn't mean—"

"You never trusted me. Not fully."

"Stop with the bullshit insinuations, Jace. That's not why you left. I'm not taking one iota of blame for anything to do with the end of our relationship, and I'm certainly not taking any blame for you *not showing up for our wedding.*" She barely kept her voice level. "*You* were the one who left *me*. You were the one that destroyed us, not me. You abandoned me on a foreign beach like some idiot, leaving me to explain to my friends and family why my fiancé vanished into thin air."

Jace dragged his hands through his hair. "I know there's nothing I can do now—or ever—to make it up to you. I just want to figure out a way forward."

"There *is* no way forward," Emily said.

"Both of us live here now. There has to be."

Emily laughed bitterly.

Jace continued, "I have to believe there's a way we can coexist in Westshore without making both our lives miserable."

"Seeing you around town doesn't make me miserable. You don't dictate my emotions anymore."

"Okay," he murmured.

The sun had fully set, painting the sky a deep violet.

"I think we're done here," Emily said, standing up.

"Okay," he repeated, but she barely heard his voice over the sound of her heartbeat and her sandals slapping the sand as she strode away.

THIRTEEN

Emily bit back the swirling emotion in her chest as she threw her car into reverse and sped home, but by the time she pulled in her driveway and reached the front door of the townhouse, she was sobbing. Her hands shook as she opened the latch to the front gate. Whether it was from relief, anger, or both, like a dam breaking, everything came out in a torrent of tears as she stumbled into the living room.

Jess rose from the couch, crossed the room, and enveloped her in a hug. Snaggles momentarily wagged by their feet, then waddled out the still-open front door.

"Everything's going to be ok," Jess said into her hair. "I promise."

"I know," Emily managed through her tears.

"You did the right thing by talking to him. You got it out. I'm proud of you."

Emily collapsed onto the couch and Jess offered her a tissue box. "Thanks." She blew her nose. "You know, I'm glad I did that. I needed to."

"Do you want to talk about anything?"

"No, I..." Emily began, and swallowed. "Not yet."

"Do you want me to stay for a while?" Jess asked.

"That would be great," Emily said, drawing her knees up to her chest.

In the silence, Emily's thoughts eased. Calmed. She let her eyes drift shut.

Untold moments later, a screech of tires tore through the night. Emily blinked.

Glancing around the kitchen and then at Jess, she asked, "Where's Snaggles?"

After Em walked away, Jason spent the next twenty minutes pacing up and down North Cove beach, replaying everything she'd said. Finally, exhausted, he'd driven home and collapsed into his favorite chair in front of the television, not even registering the Netflix teasers playing in an endless loop.

Truth be told, Jason hadn't given much thought to what Em had endured when he didn't show for their wedding in Cancún. He'd simply cut and run. Contacting airlines and hospitals? Police? He'd never taken the time to imagine how desperate her search for him might have been. And he'd been naïve to think that after finding no trace of her fiancé, Em would have been able to forget all about him. About *them*.

It wasn't until years later that Jason began to examine *why* he did what he did. Even now, after all the introspection, he was no closer to the reasons why he'd been so afraid of commitment than he was back then.

At the time, he thought Em would move on and find someone else. Jason had been sure of it, even if it took her a while. And she had.

But it was clear that that guy hadn't brought her happiness.

It was all too much to think about, too much to process right now.

Lulled by the drone of the television, Jason closed his eyes, hoping to rest for a moment or two.

The buzz of his cell phone jolted him awake, and he scrambled to find it within the cushions of the sectional couch.

"Hello?" he mumbled, blinking sleep from his eyes.

"Is this the emergency number for Williams Veterinary Clinic?"

"Yes," Jason said, trying to clear his throat. "This is Doctor Williams."

"This number is posted on the door for after-hours emergencies," a man's voice said. "My wife and I are in the parking lot of your clinic with a dog that was hit by a car—by our car. Your clinic was the closest one on Google maps."

"I'll be there in less than ten."

As Jason struggled into his sneakers, he dialed Callie and asked her to meet him at the clinic. He grabbed his keys and darted out of his apartment, glad, momentarily, for the distraction.

An elderly couple was waiting in the parking lot of the clinic, car running, an injured dog wrapped in a wool blanket on the woman's lap in the passenger seat. Jason unlocked the front door and they followed, the woman gently laying the dog on an exam table and backing away so Jason could start an examination.

"Thank you for bringing him in," Jason said. "Unfortunately, some people wouldn't even have stopped."

The front door of the clinic opened with a *swish*, and Callie appeared in the hallway behind the exam room, hair a bit disheveled, but bright-eyed. She nodded and disappeared into the back to wash up.

"We didn't even see him," the man said. "He darted right out in front of us from the side of the street. He has a collar but no name or address."

"It's okay. I'm sure we can locate his owner," Jason assured him.

"He's very sweet," the man continued. "Let Sarah here pick him up and wrap him in the blanket even though he seems to be hurt. Didn't growl or anything."

Jason slowly unwrapped the blanket. His heart sank at the sight of the little dog, whimpering, curled up, and shaking, back left leg unmoving.

"Callie," he called, trying to keep his voice steady as his stomach sank. "Would you bring in a gurney?"

The elderly woman—Sarah—burst into tears. Her husband gently put his arm around her shoulders and drew her closer.

"It looks as though he might have a broken leg, but I won't be able to see anything more until I do an x-ray," Jason said. "We'll give him some anesthesia and clean him up. You are welcome to wait, but I'm not sure there's much else for you to do at this point."

"We'll wait," the man said. Grimly, the couple made their way out to the waiting room, holding hands as they sat.

Twenty minutes later, he sent Callie into the waiting room to assure the couple that despite a few lacerations and a hairline fracture in his back leg, the little dog would be fine. Jason asked her to get the couple's contact information so he could call and update them tomorrow.

Jason looked down at the dog, drooling even while he was unconscious from the anesthesia.

Callie appeared at the door. "Mr. and Mrs. Simons just

left," she said.

"I need you to make a call for me," Jason said, pulling his cell phone out of his pocket and handing it to his tech. "Find the number for Emily Lanson in my contacts. Call her from the clinic phone and tell her Snaggles is here."

FOURTEEN

"**I** let him out the front door, but I must have forgotten to latch the front gate when I came in." Emily wiped at a tear with a shaking hand. "I wasn't thinking clearly when I got home, but I didn't think he'd wander into the street."

"Snaggles is going to be fine," the tech said with what Emily assumed to be her best assuring smile. "Doctor Williams is taking the very best care of him."

"You've been very kind," Emily replied.

Jace paused at the doorway to the waiting room and leaned against the wall, waiting. Peeking out from beneath a long white coat was the button-down shirt and jeans that he'd been wearing at the beach a few hours ago, albeit a bit rumpled as if he'd fallen asleep in them. He glanced her way, his blue eyes wary.

The usual clench in her throat was gone. Emily didn't know if that meant that their conversation eased some of the old pain, or if, because Snaggles was here, she couldn't feel anything except shock. Perhaps, like she'd said on the beach, she and Jace would never be friends. But now, seeing him, here, like this, it was somehow...*okay*.

"I'd like to keep him overnight," Jace said without preamble as his tech slipped out of the room. "The good thing is that the break wasn't bad—just a hairline fracture—and there were no other major injuries."

"Can I see him?" Emily asked.

"You can, but he's still out."

"It's okay, then." She worried her lip. "Who found him?"

"A retired couple on their way home from their daughter's house. Very nice people. They were the ones that hit him. They said they were on Pinewood Road, near Big Bend, when he darted out in front of their car."

"It's right near where I live," Emily said. "There are trees on both sides of the road and no streetlights. They probably didn't even see him."

"They called the emergency number for the clinic because it was the closest one and waited until I got here," Jace said.

"Did you get their names?"

"We did. They insisted that I call and let them know how Snaggles was doing. The wife was distraught."

"I'd like to give them a call and thank them for their kindness if you think that would be okay."

"My tech can share that number with you." He shifted his weight and stuffed his hands in his pockets. "I'll come in to check on Snaggles in the morning and let you know how he's doing." Jace paused for a second. "Is it okay if I text you after I swing by to update you on his condition?"

Nodding, Emily turned to the door. "Thank you," she said softly, and disappeared into the night without looking back.

Jess had wanted to stay with Emily overnight at the townhouse, but Emily insisted she would be fine by herself.

Instead, her best friend showed up at 6:30 the next morning—earlier than should be legal—with a bag of donuts and a tub of sliced pineapple from the grocery store down the street.

"Have you heard from Jason?" Jess asked as a bleary-eyed Emily went through the motions of making coffee.

"Not yet," Emily said around a yawn. "I thought I'd try to text him around eight. I don't know how late he was at the clinic, or how early he gets up."

Or if there's someone there when he does. And I don't want to know, thank-you-very-much.

Jess dropped her packages on the kitchen counter and started to unpack them. "I'll bet it's late enough now. He probably doesn't leave the phone on all night. Probably just turns it on when he wants to listen to messages and return calls."

"Actually, I think he leaves it on for clinic emergencies," Emily said. "That's how he got the call about Snaggles."

"The life of a professional healer," Jess said, rolling her eyes.

"The vet tech that was there last night was the woman I saw on a date with him last week at Gulf and Main. She works for him. And I swear I saw her working at Gulf and Main, too."

"That's distasteful," Jess said as she stuffed the better part of a donut into her mouth and took a gulp of coffee.

"I don't even know him anymore."

As if on cue, Emily's phone vibrated on the counter.

Snaggles is doing well. Still groggy from the anesthesia. You should be able to pick him up this afternoon. I'll have my tech contact you later today.

"Good thing I didn't block him," Emily muttered.

"There's still plenty of time for that," Jess said around another mouthful of donut. "Beach this morning? Might take your mind off things. A couple of the guys practice on Wednesdays."

"If you think a bunch of gorgeous, muscular guys playing beach volleyball is going to take my mind off things, you'd be right," Emily said.

"Speaking of gorgeous, muscular guys, are you going to see Mike again?"

"He wants to go to brunch on Sunday. I feel like I judged him too harshly—I was so surprised to see Jace there with someone, I barely paid any attention to my own date. Mike's okay, I guess," she said, spearing a piece of pineapple with a fork and picturing Jace on his date with the vet tech. "So, yeah, I think I will."

Alone at the clinic an hour after closing for the day, Jason retrieved Snaggles from the kennel in the back. The little dog was still a bit groggy, but his bottom wiggled enthusiastically when Jason took him out of the crate and out the back door to relieve himself.

Gently, he picked Snaggles up to bring him back inside and sat down in the lobby to wait for Em. Snaggles was still getting used to his cast but was making decent progress with every step.

The clinic door opened and Emily stepped inside, looking a bit worse for wear.

"Any instructions?" she asked in greeting.

Jason handed her two prescriptions. "One antibiotic and one painkiller. Directions on the bottles. He's already had both meds this morning."

"Thank you," Em murmured, picked up Snaggles, and walked out the door to her friend Jessie's car. Jason watched through the window as she settled in the passenger seat with Snaggles on her lap and Jessie shut the door before climbing in the driver's side.

Wearily, Jason locked up the clinic and drove home. As he pulled into the driveway of his condo, his cell buzzed with a text message notification.

thank you for taking care of Snaggles

He let his head fall forward against the steering wheel and let out a long breath. Making all of this work was going to be a lot harder than he thought it would be.

FIFTEEN

The Pub at Gulf and Main served the best eggs Benedict in Westshore—at least according to Mike. Emily agreed to meet him there for a brunch date, hoping he wouldn't try to convince her to *taste* the eggs Benedict—and hoping she wouldn't bump into Jace again.

She vowed not to let Jace scare her away if she did.

Jess had volunteered to stay with Snaggles, claiming she needed to work on lesson plans for the coming school year. Truthfully, the tiny dog needed help descending the stairs to the backyard enclosure; sometimes he slipped on the kitchen floor when the tip of his cast slid along the tile, his back legs splaying like Bambi on ice. Her best friend, thankfully, was more than happy to help her dog negotiate his way.

Emily glanced around the pub. Every table was full. Mike had suggested they meet at noon to beat the afternoon rush, but even if Mike was right about the eggs Benedict, he certainly hadn't been right about when the restaurant would be at its busiest.

She tapped her phone.

11:57 a.m.

Mike was dangerously close to being late.

She worried her lip.

11:58 a.m.

Emily shredded the square napkin that had been underneath her ice water.

11:59 a.m.

She texted Jess.

how's snaggles

Fine. We're watching cartoons. He likes Spongebob

thanks for watching him

Sure. Don't worry about us and have a good time.

When was Mike going to get here? Was he even going to show?

Emily fidgeted with her new shirt (she wasn't sure she liked it) and read her email on her phone (someone sold her email address to a phishing scheme again). The chair across from her moved, and she glanced up, expecting Mike.

Instead, Jace slid into the seat.

Her stomach sank.

"I just wanted to ask how Snaggles is doing this morning," he said, his eyes guarded.

Emily took a deep breath. No tightness in her throat.

Okay, then. She could do this. She *could*.

Besides, Jace was interested in her dog, not her.

"He seems all right," she said, her voice sounding rather normal to her own ears. "He has a bit of trouble walking in the kitchen, but overall, he doesn't seem to mind the cast too much."

"Is he eating and drinking okay?"

"As far as I can tell," Emily said. She took another deep breath, steeling herself for what she was about to say. "I need to apologize to you."

His eyebrow lifted. "How so?"

"I'm sorry for being rude when I first bumped into you— actually, the first couple times I saw you in town. Storming out of bars and veterinary clinics aren't things I usually do. I didn't mean to assume anything about your life. It's not my business."

"Okay," he said, his eyes still wary.

"I don't want to play this high school avoidance thing anymore. It's stupid. It's been eight years. I've said my peace. I need to live my life and not worry if I'm going to bump into you in the grocery store or at the gas station. I'd like for us to be on civil terms, if we can." Emily said.

Jace nodded. "Me, too."

"You've been kind and patient. And I've been...angry. I've been angry for so long that I didn't know how else to react to you. I didn't mean—"

Mike suddenly appeared next to Jace. "That's my seat," he said, crossing his arms with a deadly smile and a hint of malice that made Emily cringe.

Jace stood up. "Absolutely," he said levelly. "Good to see you, Em," he said. As he turned to walk away, Mike stepped in his way, partially blocking his path so that they bumped shoulders.

Great. A pissing match between two gorillas. Just what I need to brighten my Sunday afternoon.

Mike's face darkened as his gaze followed Jace as he walked toward the bar and started a conversation with the owner.

"How do you know that asshole?"

"He's my veterinarian," Emily said. "Snaggles got hit by a

car and broke his leg. He was checking in with me to see how he was doing."

"Maybe he should check in someplace other than a bar," Mike said. "Maybe at his office, for instance."

He sat down. A moment later, Mike seemed to shake it off.

The food at Gulf and Main—a fruit plate with a side of granola, in Emily's case—was as good as rumored. Mike seemed willing to engage in, well, *somewhat* engaging conversation, and, for a moment or two, she forgot about a certain vanishing, lying ex-fiancé.

As a plus, she successfully avoided the eggs Benedict.

All in all, a successful date.

It wasn't until she was driving away that she realized Mike had never asked how Snaggles was doing.

SIXTEEN

Jason climbed into Tyler's truck and nodded a grateful hello. His cousin had agreed to swing by and pick him up on the way to South Cove for a game of beach volleyball. Getting out of his condo might help alleviate his sour mood, even if he wasn't big on the idea of getting sand up the crack of his ass.

Tyler had been pestering Jason for years to join him for an occasional game or two of volleyball. With the clinic closed for Memorial Day—and Tyler just back from Africa—Jason had no excuse for blowing it off. Well, no excuse that Tyler would accept.

Keeping his thoughts from wandering to Em would be a nice side benefit.

Even now, too many things still bounced around Jason's head from his conversation with Em at the beach. Seeing her anger and disgust—and then her pain at Snaggles' injury—ripped him up inside in ways he'd never felt before.

Truthfully, Jason also wanted to circle back with Tyler to let him know he'd apologized to Em face to face. He'd done what his cousin had suggested: kept his mouth shut and let her say everything she needed to say. Now, maybe he could move forward. *They* could move forward.

Somehow.

Jason took a deep breath. "I talked to Em last week," he said.

Tyler nodded as he backed out of Jason's driveway. "How was that?"

"Could have been better. Could have been worse. I took your advice—I let her speak her peace. And I apologized, of course."

"Of course," Tyler echoed. "Besides being blindsided by your presence in Westshore Beach, how is she?"

"Well, her rescue was hit by a car and wound up at my clinic at 1 a.m. that night. The people who hit the dog happened to be close to the clinic and called the emergency number. I knew when they brought him inside that it was her dog."

"Damn," Tyler muttered. "The universe is working overtime to get you two in the same room together to sort things out."

"Did the lion scat make you some kind of a mystic, too?"

"No. It's just obvious if you're sitting on the outside looking in," Tyler said levelly.

"Well, the dog will be fine. Em on the other hand..." Jason shook his head in dismay.

While they waited at the red light to the road leading to the beach access, Tyler turned to Jason. "You've got to let her be, man," he said. "It's the best thing to do right now."

They finished the trip to South Cove in silence.

Tyler pulled into the municipal parking lot and pulled their gear out of the back of his car.

"Hey, gorgeous," a woman called. She was in a beach chair off to the side of the makeshift volleyball court and was peeking over her book, eyes only for Tyler. *Jessie.*

Another reason Jason had never come to volleyball.

"Hey, yourself," Tyler called back.

His cousin sauntered over, drew Em's best friend out of her chair, and wrapped his arms around her. She giggled. The two lingered in their embrace as he nuzzled her neck.

Jason glanced around. Three women in string bikinis were arranging their chairs a few paces behind Jessie. One winked at him when she caught him looking.

Good Lord. Are those groupies waiting for the guys to play?

After a solid minute—right when Jason was about to tell Tyler and Jessie to get a room—Tyler pulled away. While still gazing adoringly at Jessie, he said, "You remember my cousin, Jason."

Looking around Tyler's shoulder, Jessie said, "Sure do."

Jason huffed a bitter laugh. How could she not? He'd ripped out her best friend's heart and stranded it on a beach on the other side of the Gulf of Mexico. Not the easiest thing to forget. Or, maybe, forgive.

"Does he know what he's in for today?" Jessie said, glancing up at Tyler.

His cousin grunted noncommittally and gave Jessie a wry smile.

"It's probably for the best," she added.

Two guys sauntered toward the poles, dropped a nylon bag in the sand, and began unwinding a black net to stretch across the sand court. One was long, lean, and at least three inches taller than Jason, and very likely younger. Jason was no slouch, but he was more of a gym rat than someone who'd enjoyed a weekly game of batting a ball into the air with his hands.

One of them nodded in greeting—his ponytail bobbing in time with his chin—while the other appraised him openly.

Wait, that was—

The dick Em had been on a date with at Gulf and Main.

Fabulous. So glad I came.

Jason squinted down the beach. The eleven o'clock summer sun burned along his skin, reminding him he hadn't seen the midday sun for weeks and making him even more thankful he was wearing a baseball hat. "You don't happen to have any sunscreen, do you?" he asked Jessie.

She dug around in her bag, produced a tube, and tossed it to him. He caught it with one hand and started in on his shoulders.

Tyler glanced at the guys attaching the net to the poles. "Malone can be a bit of a prick, but the other guys are generally all right. Not sure who's showing up today, though, since it's a holiday."

"Good enough," Jason replied as he followed Tyler over to the court.

"This is my cousin, Jason. Take it easy on him, will you?" Tyler said, nodding his head in Jason's direction.

They chuckled, shifting on their feet. Ponytail-guy began to throw the volleyball in the air, catching it and tossing it up again.

"Whatever you say, Dawson," said the dark-haired one snidely.

Jason took his spot on the side next to his cousin, and the dark-haired guy—Malone, apparently—served the ball, spiking it down a foot in front of Jason before he could react and sending sand flying in all directions.

The women behind Jess raised their beers in a congratulatory salute.

Some distractions, Jason thought as he brushed the sand off his sunglasses, *just aren't worth it.*

Emily had always known that she'd hit the proverbial lottery on mothers. Wisdom crystalized into nuggets of no-nonsense advice was her mom's specialty, and if there was any time when she needed counsel without a sugar coating, it was right now.

As Emily eased her car into the driveway of the beach bungalow, she could see her mom on the sandy beach out beyond the deck. Her mom's gaze was fixed on the gulf, Birkenstock sandals in one hand, and a glass of wine in the other.

"Better not let the cops see you with glass on the beach," Emily said as she approached, greeting her mom with a smile.

Chuckling, her mom said, "That's exactly what I'm hoping—to be accosted by a tall, dark, and handsome policeman." She waggled her eyebrows. "Obviously, I require private instruction on the particulars of the law as it applies to old women who enjoy Cabernet and douse themselves in patchouli."

Emily laughed.

They stood for a moment side by side staring into the horizon, the comfortable silence broken only by the tinkling of broken shells as they were tossed along the edge of the gulf's gentle waves.

"The postcard…"

Her mother cocked her head as if considering Emily's words and then a flash of understanding passed over her face. "Oh, honey."

"Yeah." It was all Emily could manage before her voice failed her.

"Let's walk," her mom said, throwing her sandals toward the deck stairs and missing terribly.

They started down the beach as the sun slipped toward

the horizon.

"Have you seen him?" her mom asked.

"I bumped into him when I picked up Snaggles after he got his teeth cleaned," Emily said. "And the other night, Snaggles escaped the front fence and was hit by a car. The people who hit him took him to Jace's clinic."

"Is Snaggles okay?"

"Just a hairline fracture in his back leg. He'll be fine."

Her mom nodded and absorbed Emily's news in silence.

"So, you've seen Jason and interacted with him. But have you spoken with him?"

"Of course, I mean how could I have not—"

"No, Em. Have you *spoken* with him?"

Emily sighed. "Yeah. We met the other day, and I said *all the things.*"

Her mom made a noncommittal sound.

They continued their stroll down the beach, pausing occasionally while her mom sifted through the tiny treasures gifted from the melancholy sea.

"Are you still angry about what happened? What he did?" her mom asked.

"I'm not sure. I think so. I tried getting past it, but I've lived with it for so long..." Emily shrugged. "I'm sure there are things I forgot to say when I met with him. Maybe it will take more than one conversation to get it all sorted out."

"Maybe."

Emily sighed. "Part of me still wants to be mad."

"And that's okay. You get to take as much time as you like." Her mom picked up a welk and turned it over, then met Emily's eye with a sad smile. "Thing is, though, it's much easier on you and your psyche to let go of anger. I'm sure you've heard that it's much better in the long run." She slipped the shell into her pocket. "When it doesn't serve you any longer, let it go."

Emily rolled her eyes. "I'm not a Disney princess, mom."

"Maybe not, but it's still decent advice for all of us," her mom said. "You've said your peace and he was receptive, right?"

Emily nodded.

"So, you've said your peace. Now *make* peace," she said. "Those are two different things."

"How can I make peace with what he did?"

"It's less about making peace with what he did than making peace with what's inside you."

"I don't understand," Emily said.

"I know why this still hurts so badly," her mom said levelly.

"Let me guess," Emily said snidely. "It's because Jace basically left me at the altar. Except in this case, the altar was a beach on the other side of the Gulf of Mexico."

"No, sweetie. That's the biggest part of it, but that's not all of it." Her mom paused for a moment, set her glass on the sand, and folded her hands around Emily's, her bright eyes welling with tears. "It's because of your dad."

"What do you mean?"

"When your dad was killed, you didn't get to say goodbye."

Emily blinked. "You didn't get to say goodbye either. None of us did."

"True. But you were the one who needed closure the most." After retrieving her glass from the sand, her mom started down the beach again. "You haven't made the connection, have you? You were just seven years old the day your dad died. He was supposed to pick you up—and he never did. When you got to the hospital after the crash—"

Emily shook the memory away. "But Dad didn't

127

intentionally do that."

"You're right, he didn't." Her mom offered another sad smile. "Your dad didn't choose to disappear, and Jason did. But that doesn't truly matter, does it? What matters is that neither of them showed up. They left without saying goodbye."

Emily tried to reconcile her mom's words with how she felt about Jace. It was—

"When you're ready, make peace," her mom said, taking her hand. "And do it for you."

SEVENTEEN

Three weeks of weekly visits.

Three weeks of torture of the worst kind. Or possibly the best.

And there were three weeks to go.

Despite Jason's assurance that any vet in Westshore could handle the follow-ups after Snaggle's injury, Em had insisted on bringing Snaggles exclusively to him. Jason couldn't fathom why. The little dog was progressing well, and now there were only a handful visits left before the cast on his leg would be removed.

The first time Em had come to the clinic with Snaggles, she'd brought Jessie with her. Her best friend had stood silently at his ex's side despite the pall of awkwardness that settled over the exam room. But since that visit, Em had come alone. The second week, she'd been stoic and civil. No surprise there—based on what she'd said at the beach, he knew that she would never allow a friendship to grow between them.

The knowledge filled him with a profound sense of loss.

Despite everything, Jason found himself counting down

the days until Em showed up for Snaggles' next appointment.

Last week, he'd sworn he'd seen a smile tug her lips when she was looking at Snaggles.

And today, he'd sworn Em had almost smiled at *him*.

Progress. *Maybe.*

Jason kept his eyes on Em as she strode out of the exam room and toward the front door of the clinic, Snaggles at the end of a thin leash at her side. As much as he tried, he couldn't tear his gaze from her. There was an overwhelming urge—an insatiable need—to watch her as long as he could.

Something he didn't want to examine twisted in his chest as the glass door closed behind her with a *swoosh*. Something he didn't want to name.

He turned to see Callie guiding Mrs. Selby and Tootles into Exam Room Four.

Flipping through a clipboard, Jason stepped into the room, planting a smile on his face that he was certain didn't touch his eyes. "Good morning, Mrs. Selby," he said. Jason bent down to greet the Pomeranian. "Feeling under the weather, little guy?"

"There's nothing wrong with Tootles," she answered crisply.

"Forgive me, Mrs. Selby," he said. "Did you say that there was nothing wrong with Tootles?"

Before answering, she paused momentarily. "As you know, I come here quite a bit. I enjoy getting out of my house and seeing friendly faces like yours." She sighed. "My husband is gone. Most of my friends are gone. We were never able to have children…" She shook her head as if shaking away a particularly painful memory. "And yes, a time or two when I've come, there has been something amiss with Tootles. But not today."

"Mrs. Selby—"

"May I ask you something of a personal nature, Doctor Williams?"

He dropped down onto one of the plastic molded chairs across from her, setting the clipboard aside. "Absolutely."

The elderly woman folded her knobby hands in her lap. "On second thought, perhaps I have an observation rather than a question."

Jason raised an eyebrow.

"No. It's not an observation, either," she amended, mostly to herself. She met Jason's eye. "It seems I'm here to tell you a story."

He gave her an encouraging nod.

"A very long time ago, a boy fell in love with a girl. He decided to court her, but he didn't have much money. Oh, he was a hard worker, that boy, and he was busy saving every penny he could for the future he imagined with the girl.

"Every day on his way to visit her that first summer, he would trim a rose bloom from his mother's bushes—not too far down, as to not hurt the plant, you see. But in all his excitement to give it to her, he would forget to cut the thorns off."

Jason wondered where on earth she was going with this.

"In that way, the girl received rose after rose. Short stems. Thorns. But they were the most beautiful peach color the girl had ever seen, soft as a gentle Florida sunset and fragrant as an entire meadow in spring."

Mrs. Selby glanced down at her peach dress.

"One day that winter, when the boy had a bit of extra money, he decided to buy her a rose from a florist shop. A proper rose, in the middle of winter. A long-stemmed, thorn-free rose. One, he imagined, the girl would be proud of. One that meant he had enough extra money to *buy* roses, rather than cutting them from his mother's bushes in the backyard.

"But the florist didn't carry peach-colored roses," she said, fingering her fake corsage. "So, the boy bought the closest thing—yellow ones. And when the boy handed the girl the single yellow rose that winter day, her heart fell."

Mrs. Selby looked at him meaningfully.

Jason frowned. "I don't understand."

"Are you familiar with floriography, Doctor Williams?"

"No," he said. "I haven't heard that word before."

"Floriography is language expressed in flowers. In Victorian times, flowers were employed to communicate all sorts of things. It was a quite serious endeavor. Books were published about it. In fact, the first widely used dictionary of floriography, *La Langage des Fleurs,* was written by Louis Cortambert in 1819.

"No matter," she continued. "Back to my story. The boy, much like you, had no knowledge of floriography. But the girl, like most girls at the time, knew it well. She believed that flowers expressed specific things. For example, orange or peach roses meant desire and enthusiasm."

Mrs. Selby locked her weepy eyes on Jason's and squared her shoulders.

"And yellow roses mean friendship."

"But the boy—" Jason began.

"The boy persisted in bringing her yellow roses all winter. Of course, the boy was unaware of the message he was sending. The girl grew confused, then set her hopes on another."

She leaned down to scratch Tootles behind his ears.

"It wasn't until I'd—*she'd* almost married another that the girl discovered the error of what she believed."

She fingered her corsage again.

"My husband loved me beyond measure, as I loved him." She met Jason's eye. "I miss him every minute of every day.

He bought me peach roses every week for nearly sixty years."

"Mrs. Selby—"

"You know that woman that just left with the pitifully ugly dog, don't you? From somewhere other than here?"

Jason nodded slowly. "I do."

"I was in the waiting room when she left, and I saw her face. And I saw yours. I saw how miserable you both are when you walk away from each other," she said. "Don't lose her over a misunderstanding, like I almost lost my husband."

"I'm afraid it's bigger than a misunderstanding, Mrs. Selby."

She stood, tucking her purse under her arm and straightening her dress. Tootles got up and waited, looking up at his owner expectantly.

"Nothing, my dear boy, is ever bigger than a misunderstanding." She walked to the door of the exam room, Tootles waddling alongside her.

"That ship has sailed, Mrs. Selby," he said sadly.

She paused, hand on the doorknob. "Are you certain, Doctor Williams? Absolutely certain?"

"I—"

"If you love her beyond measure, as I suspect you do, make sure she knows that. The last thing you want to do is look back and wonder if there was more you could have said or done. Heaven forbid that she believes something that isn't true."

Still processing Mrs. Selby's words, Jason made his way to the reception desk. The clinic phone rang, and Kathleen swiveled to answer it.

After a moment she said, "The best place would be Westshore Animal Shelter. I can give you their number—"

Kathleen glanced up and met Jason's eye.

"May I put you on hold?" she asked.

She turned to Jason. "There's a woman on the phone who found a Lab and a litter of five newborn pups under her deck when she got back from vacation," she said. "Looks like the mom is a stray. She's already called Westshore Animal Shelter but they're full. They're turning away everyone, apparently. She called to see if there was anything we could do to help."

"Let me talk to her," Jason said, sliding into the chair next to Kathleen.

He picked up the phone. "Hello? This is Doctor Williams. Where are the mom and pups right now?"

"She's made a little den under our deck in the backyard," the woman said.

And the next thing he knew, Jason was in his car, headed toward downtown, Mrs. Selby's words still echoing around in his head.

Three hours later, a section of Jason's living room was partitioned behind a dog gate, and the mother and her pups were sleeping off the excitement of the afternoon's move. The room wasn't being used all that often anyway, and Jason was more than happy to provide a temporary home for the new family at the cost of a bit of living space.

It would be nice to have a reason to come home other than a baseball game on television.

The newborn puppies snuggled up next to their mother. The largest of the five twitched in his sleep, then stretched lazily.

"Hey, little guy," he said to the puppy, stroking his fur.

Jason smiled. This, *this* felt right. He hadn't realized how empty the condo felt until he'd brought home the Lab and her puppies. Now it seemed a little more like a home.

Sure, he'd brought a dog or two home to foster for a few weeks when the need arose, before finding them a forever home. Never a family.

The right dog for him hadn't come along yet.

Watching the mother sleeping soundly, he wondered if he hadn't just found one.

After eating a late dinner alone and catching up on email, Jason still couldn't get the conversation with Mrs. Selby out of his mind.

Did he still, in Mrs. Selby's words, love Em beyond measure?

Yes, he realized. *A million times, yes.*

What if he looked back in a week, a month, or a year and realized there was more he could have done to repair what had happened? Could he live with himself if he let her slip away again?

There were only three more appointments before Snaggles' cast would be removed. If he was going to act, he needed to do it now.

And a certain chatty part-time vet tech had mentioned in passing exactly where Jason might find Em on Sunday afternoons.

I could wait for her to approach me. Be available but let her make the first move.

From across the room, the Lab barked to be let out. The condo was small enough when it was only him, and now, with the addition of five dogs, it would soon be as chaotic as a mosh pit. If he was serious about keeping her, and potentially one of the puppies, he was going to need a bigger place. And soon.

After returning from walking the dog, Jason opened his

laptop and searched for properties in Westshore Beach that were for sale. Something cozy and old—maybe something he could fix up, if needed—was fine, even preferable, as long as it was near the beach. At least if he had a yard or a deck, there'd be more space than in his one-bedroom condo.

Jason messaged a real estate agent and made an appointment to meet her at Gulf and Main a week from Sunday. Maybe he'd even steal a glance at Em while he was there.

It was past time for a change—another distraction.

And he was a veritable expert in distractions, wasn't he?

EIGHTEEN

Somehow, every single Sunday when Emily walked into Gulf and Main to wait for Mike to arrive for their weekly brunch date, Jace was already there.

He'd be alone, parked at the bar staring at an untouched plate of food cooling in front of him. Periodically, one of the bartenders would pause their work to chat, their faces lighting up under Jace's perfect attention.

Emily did her best not to watch.

She failed every single time.

And somehow, the earlier Emily arrived, the earlier Jace would arrive the following week. Last Sunday, Gulf and Main wasn't even open when they arrived.

At exactly eleven o'clock, Cassidy had unlocked the front door, and Emily waited in her car until Jace walked inside. She gave him precisely three minutes to settle in. By the time she'd crossed the pub's threshold, Jace was seated at his favorite stool and pretending the menu was something he'd never read before.

Emily chose the same booth in the back corner each week, the one closest to the hallway leading to the restrooms.

Occasionally, Jace would stroll past her table before turning down the hall. He'd nod or give her a tentative smile. He might stop by her booth on his way back, to ask how Snaggles was faring or to offer a benign comment on the weather. He'd always be parked back at the bar long before Mike showed up for another one of their weekly brunch dates.

At least Jace was trying.

It was more than she could say for herself.

The conversations with Jace on his way to and from the restroom had begun to move from acceptably civil to a tiny bit more friendly. At first, he'd acted stiff and cordial, almost as if he were someone she'd never met before, but as the weeks rolled on, she sensed a change.

Lingering by the booth a little longer than the Sunday before.

A smile, a touch warmer than the week before.

The smallest hesitation before he walked away, as if he wanted to stay but didn't know how.

Today, she decided that she would walk over and talk to him. Like a normal person. Because if he could do it, so could she.

Emily glanced at her cell.

10:47 a.m.

Plenty of time to chat before Mike arrived. She could initiate a conversation with Jace. She could do it. She *could*.

Taking a deep breath, Emily rose from her booth, strode over to the bar, and sat down next to her ex-fiancé. Jace pushed his untouched food away and focused his perfect attention on her.

She'd forgotten how it felt to be the sole object of his notice. She swallowed. Hard.

I refuse to get lost in Jason Disappearing Act Williams' eyes.

"On the house," the bartender said, sliding two drinks across the bar with a crooked smile.

"Now I know how you get all your drinks," Emily managed. "You find all the bartenders in town that own dogs and cats, and you charm them with your veterinary expertise. *Voilà*, free margaritas for life."

"An unexpected perk," Jace said with a wry smile. "Not that I go out all that much, but Cass insists."

Cassidy chuckled and moved on to another customer at the other end of the bar. Jason watched her go.

"You do seem to manage to go out every Sunday afternoon," Emily said.

He lifted an eyebrow. "I do," he said, fixing his attention back on her.

Now, one gaze in her direction, and her belly dove into freefall.

Fabulous.

"What's been keeping you busy lately?" she asked.

Lame, she chided herself. *You couldn't make adult conversation if your life depended on it.*

"I'm thinking of moving," Jace said. "I need a bigger place. And I'd like to be closer to the beach."

That voice.

Emily had always loved Jace's voice.

It was chocolate and cinnamon and it reverberated deep within her, suggesting things that she should *not* be thinking. Or imagining. Or longing for—

Dammit.

"Why live in Westshore if you're not near the beach?" Emily managed.

"Exactly."

"I rented my townhouse sight unseen," she continued, pushing the salt lining on the rim of her margarita into the drink to keep herself from staring at Jace. "Now that I'm here, I can take my time looking for a more permanent place. Plus, I think it'd be a good idea to get Snaggles as far away from Big Bend as I can."

"I'd do the same thing," he said. "I'm going to start looking at what's available. I'm meeting my real estate agent here every Sunday at 1:30 so she can take me around to potential properties."

"I guess I'll see you here, then. Mike and I meet here for Sunday brunch at noon every week. It's tradition." Emily said, knowing full well Jace was more than aware of her weekend agenda. She glanced at her cell. "I'm a bit early, as usual."

Jace took a long swallow of his drink. "Already creating traditions, huh? How long have you been seeing each other?"

Emily hesitated as a flare of anger heated her face. She might be attracted to her ex-fiancé—honestly, who wouldn't be? —but that was none of his business. Instead of answering Jace's question, she said, "He knows it's important to me, so he does his part and shows up."

Jace snapped his mouth shut.

Maybe he didn't deserve that. Or maybe he did.

Keep your shit together, Emily. It doesn't matter anymore. He apologized. And besides, you were the one that sat down next to him.

Emily took a long breath. Jace wasn't being nosey or judgmental. He was just making conversation. He didn't mean anything by it. Right? Right.

The front door opened. Emilly turned, her smile faltering a fraction. "Mike's here," she said, rising from the barstool. "Best of luck with your search," she said, standing. She didn't wait for his reply.

She forced her feet toward her booth and sat back down with a sigh. How did that man manage to tangle her emotions into knots? First, she was imagining his voice murmuring deliciously in her ear, and next she was snapping at him for asking about Mike. She seriously needed to get a grip.

"You're here early," Emily said as he pulled out a chair.

He nodded toward the bar. "Isn't that your vet?"

"It is. I just said hi to him."

"I don't know why you talk to that guy," he said, a frown creasing his brow.

"He's great with Snaggles."

Mike shrugged and waved Callie over to order a Bloody Mary.

"I'm going out of town," he said, turning back to Emily. "Quarterly company meeting next week. I'm going early, so I won't be here for brunch next Sunday."

"Where's the meeting?"

"Vegas."

"That should be fun," Emily said.

Mike nodded. "Training all day. Playing all night." A cocky smile. "My boys know how to enjoy themselves."

Emily glanced over Mike's shoulder at the bartender talking with Jace. Her chest tightened.

"I know we've been doing this brunch thing for a while because I work late most nights," Mike began.

"It's okay with me. Really. It's no big deal. I'm sure we'll get a chance to go to dinner or a movie—or whatever—when you've got more time."

"We will. But I thought since we'll miss next Sunday's brunch, we could have drinks here on Friday night. I'm planning on taking the night off, at least from work."

"Sounds great."

"In the meantime, I want to tell you about my goal, Miss Vegan." Mike wiped his mouth on a napkin and slid closer, sneaking his arm around the back of her chair and looking rather pleased with himself.

She blinked. "Goal?"

He leaned into her ear, close enough that she could feel his hot breath, and whispered, "Get you sloppy drunk and feed you a hamburger with my fingers while you moan in—"

Thankfully, the bartender chose that moment to stop at their table with Mike's drink. "Another round?" she asked, nodding at Emily's near-empty margarita.

Emily managed a smile. "I'm good."

And she was, until a woman wearing a name tag on her lapel and an indecently short skirt settled into the barstool next to Jace.

NINETEEN

"It's been on the market for two days."

Jason's new real estate agent, Amanda Brockton, paged through her notebook until she found the entry she was looking for. "It's an older cottage, but it's been lovingly cared for," she continued. "The couple selling it has lived here for over thirty years."

Jason nodded as he wandered the kitchen. The cottage was the third property she'd taken him to that afternoon. Out of all the prospects—including the five they viewed the Sunday before—it was by far his favorite.

"It was appraised last year. The price is right in line with appraised value," she said, eyeing him over her notes.

It was the second time he'd caught her appraising *him* when she thought he wasn't looking.

Maybe this week her skirt had been a bit shorter than last week.

Not that he was complaining. Not at all.

Amanda was gorgeous, with legs for miles, creamy skin, and full lips that craved attention.

Jason glanced down the hall. The cottage was a two-bedroom, one-and-a-half-bath gem. The main room had built-in bookshelves covering the entire north wall and the kitchen had been updated with new white cabinets and granite countertops, recessed lights, and a large farmhouse sink.

The moment Jason had stepped through the front door, he knew it was his next home.

"I'd like to put in a cash offer," he said.

Amanda's eyebrows rose before she blinked the surprise away. "Would you like to see the rest of the cottage first? Maybe see how large the bedrooms are?"

"I'm sure they're big enough for anything that I might be interested in doing in there," he quipped.

"Hmmm…" she said, putting her notebook back in her purse and sauntering over, the edges of her lips tilting upward. "Perhaps we should make sure."

Ten days later, Jason was at a title company's office signing a whirlwind of papers to make the cottage his own.

"Congratulations," Amanda said when it was all over, her handshake lingering just a breath too long as the room emptied. "Who will you be celebrating with?"

A bit of a personal question, surely, but with the way she'd been eyeing him for weeks, Jason wasn't surprised. His closest friends, Callie, Mel, Cass, Kathleen, and Tyler—with Jessie in tow, no doubt—they'd celebrate with him, certainly. They'd gather at the cottage, toast to his new place, grill a couple of steaks, and when it was all over, they'd go back to their homes and hold their partners close and talk about how much fun they had.

Which was something he couldn't do because the one person he wanted to celebrate with the most was gone.

And it was his fault.

"I'll likely be celebrating alone," he said levelly.

Something sparkled in Amanda's eyes. "Well, I'm prepared to help out with that, too. If you're game, that is."

A nice diversion in the form of legs for miles would be quite welcome. It might even help him forget about Em for, well, a minute. Or two, at most.

Well, at least he and Amanda were on the same page.

He shrugged. "Why the hell not?"

"So. How long have you lived in Westshore Beach?"

Jason's one-time real estate agent, now *potential distraction,* watched him over the rim of her wine glass, surveying him with a barely restrained, hazel-eyed hunger.

Ah, the ever-so-polite, let's-get-to-know-each-other questions. Here we go.

Amanda turned out to be a master of pleasantries. No surprise there; as a real estate agent she was probably used to making small talk, asking the trite but expected questions to get a fledgling relationship going.

But despite her obvious experience, dinner was an hour and forty-five minutes of largely unremarkable conversation. Jason discovered where she had relocated from (Columbus, Ohio), how long she'd been a real estate agent (six years), and how many pets she had (none).

Amanda was stunning but nothing else about her remotely interested him. When they finished dessert, even Amanda had run out of conversation starters.

Maybe he'd be game for a no-strings-attached romp. It had been longer than he cared to remember since he'd gone looking for that kind of evening, and she seemed, well, more than willing.

Time to salvage what was left of their date.

"I was thinking—" he began.

She raised a hopeful eyebrow, her lips twisting in anticipation.

"Maybe we could have a nightcap?"

"That sounds deliciously old-fashioned and, I must say, rather desirable," she purred. "Charming, even."

"There's a place downtown that I like to go—a small place, mostly locals. Not fancy. I happen to know the owner," he said.

Half an hour later, Jason was holding the door open for Amanda at Gulf and Main. When she excused herself to the restroom, Callie appeared behind the bar.

"Nope," she said while pouring another glass of wine for Amanda. "Nope, nope, nope."

"Come on, Callie," Jason whispered, leaning in. "This is my first date in ages. You can't do that to me."

"She's not for you. I can tell, remember?"

"Are you going to tell me who *is* for me?"

Callie pursed her lips. "Look, it's complicated. I'm working on it."

Amanda returned in a fresh coat of lipstick and slid into the stool next to Jason, slowly crossing her long legs.

"You're one of the fastest deals I ever made," Amanda said. She cocked her head to the side and raised an eyebrow. "And I like fast." He saw her eyes light in anticipation.

"I guess when you know, you know," Jason said.

"Would you like to put in any other offers tonight?" she asked, tracing her index finger along the rim of her wine glass.

Well, that was straight to the point.

He glanced over at Callie, who was filling a blender with ice, still shaking her head.

"I had a great time, Amanda," Jason began, forcing the

rest of the words out. "You're gorgeous and sweet, and I loved spending the evening with you. But I just don't think it is going to work out."

"This is when you say, 'it's not you, it's me,'" Amanda said.

"It *is* me," Jason said.

"I'm going to go," Amanda said, standing.

He nodded at their mostly full glasses. "Are you sure? We could finish our—"

"That's okay." She glanced around the bar. "It was great getting to know you, Jason."

As Jason drove home, all he could do was wonder if he'd ever find someone he'd want as much as he still wanted Em.

TWENTY

The following Sunday, Jason planted himself at the bar at Gulf and Main the second it opened. As usual, Emily wandered in several minutes later and settled into her customary corner booth.

He winked at Callie as she darted from table to table taking orders and she winked back.

"Don't be scared, Boss, but I think it's time I told you about your perfect match," she said, leaning over the bar toward him when she had a free moment to say hello.

"Oh, really?"

"I've been thinking about it. She's the one I spoke to in the bathroom here a few weeks ago."

"Finding me hot dates in the restroom of Gulf and Main, huh? Did you scrawl my number in every stall?"

Callie offered him a dimpled smile. "I won't even describe her because it doesn't matter what she looks like. She's, well, she's the right one. I can feel it. You guys belong together."

"You can feel it?"

"Yup." She poured him a cup of coffee and set the cream

and sugar in front of him. "And it certainly wasn't that woman you brought here the other night, dressed like she would rather be at the Ritz."

"You mean Amanda, my real estate agent."

"I don't know. All I know is that you need to run away far, far from that one."

Jason sighed. "Consider it done."

Callie gifted him one of her billion wattage smiles.

"So, when are you going to introduce me to my perfect match?" Jason asked.

"I'll tell you when I see her next." Callie winked and disappeared into the back.

Jason contemplated his coffee.

The barstool next to him moved and Em dropped down into it, a brown bag of takeout in her hand. He blinked.

"Hey," she said, as if settling down at the bar next to Jason was something she did every day.

"Hey," Jason managed.

"What's new?"

"Uh…" Did he ever do anything new? "Well, I bought a house."

"That's big news," she said. "Congratulations."

"Thanks. You should swing by and—" Jason stopped, hung his head, and chuckled. "Sorry. Sometimes I forget that we're not—" He took a deep breath. "I know you don't want to be friends."

"It's okay."

Neither spoke for a minute.

"Maybe we could figure out how to be," Em said.

"Uh—"

"Look, I just stopped in for a sec. I'm supposed to meet Jess, so I have to get going."

As Em left, Callie reappeared at the other side of the bar

and leaned toward him, whispering, "That's her."

"Who?"

"The woman you were talking to. That's your perfect match."

Jason's heart faltered. "Callie—"

His friend offered up another one of her devastatingly beautiful smiles. "You should have told me you already knew her."

He took a shaky breath and stood, raking his fingers through his hair.

"Taking off?" Callie asked.

"Yeah," Jason said, fishing his wallet out of his back pocket and laying a ten on the bar.

"You know I'm not allowed to charge you for the coffee, Boss," she said, sliding the money back toward him.

"And you know you're not allowed to call me 'Boss'," he said, sliding it back.

"So many rules."

"My cousin is stopping by my new place. I'm going to show him the puppies, so I have to run."

Callie started to say something, and then nodded. "Sometime you're going to have to explain to me what's going on between you and Miss Perfect for You."

Jason pursed his lips and let a long breath out through his nose. "If I ever figure it out, you'll be the first to know."

Half an hour later, Jason opened the front door of his cottage, and invited Tyler inside with a smile. Five sleepy-eyed puppies stretched awake and scrambled for the door.

"I like it," Tyler said, glancing around. "Nice view. Great deck. And close to the state park."

"Thanks. Once I get the rest of my stuff over from the

condo and unpacked, it will feel more like home."

Tyler nodded at Molly and the puppies swarming around his feet. "These must be the pups you're fostering."

"Yeah. The Lab was a stray. Westshore shelter was full, so I took them in."

"Are you going to keep all of them?"

"Just the big guy, Flint. My receptionist is taking the other male. I'll keep the mom, too. I named her Molly," Jason said.

Tyler bent down to scratch one of the puppy's bellies; Molly sniffed his cowboy boots as if they were the most interesting things in the world.

"How many animals do you have at your place now?" Jason asked.

"Just the bay gelding and the red dun mare. I've still got a couple of kids taking care of them whenever I travel. They do a good job."

"I'm guessing Jessie wants one, doesn't she?" Jason asked, chuckling at the puppy as its back leg wiggled in time with Tyler's scratches.

"She does. A female."

Jason squatted down next to the puppy. "This one is the smartest of the lot. I've been calling her Sadie."

His cousin nodded and stood up. "That one will work."

Jason raised an eyebrow. "And somehow you keep telling me there isn't anything going on between you two. As if you didn't come over here to approve."

Tyler huffed a laugh. "Maybe, I did. Maybe I didn't."

"I can't believe someone just left this dog," Jason said. "Dogs are emotional creatures. They hurt when the people who love them disappear. She's chipped, which means someone loved her once. The owner finally called me back after I left a ton of messages, saying he didn't want her anymore. From this dog's point of view, the person she loved most in the world just vanished."

Tyler stared at him and said nothing.

"What?" Jason asked.

"Do you hear yourself?"

Jason raised an eyebrow.

"'The person she loved most in the world just vanished.'," Tyler repeated.

Jason grunted. Leave it to his cousin to see something he couldn't.

"Right," Jason said, frowning.

"Hey," Tyler said, straightening and giving Jason a thump on the shoulder, "whenever you can recognize when you're being a hypocrite, that's progress."

Nauseous.

That's what it felt like simply contemplating telling her best friend about what Mike had said on their last brunch date. But she had to tell someone. Besides, Jess had hounded Emily for details on how things were going between her and Mike, and this one little sentence would tell Jess all she needed to know.

Emily and Jess were happily ensconced in their beach chairs underneath a striped umbrella, the breeze and lack of clouds suggesting the coming afternoon would be scorching.

Keeping her eyes on the couple strolling by hand in hand along the water, Emily took a deep breath. "Mike told me his goal was going to get me drunk and feed me a hamburger."

Jess shuddered elegantly. "What? Seriously? That's gross. What an asshole."

"That guy's got balls," Emily said. "That's for sure."

"But think of how magnificent they are," Jess breathed.

"Jess!"

"I'm *kidding*," Jess said. "His balls have no bearing on this conversation." She cleared her throat. "Balls. Bearing. See what I did there?"

Emily rolled her eyes.

"Listen, Em. Seriously, now. Seriously. He basically told you outright that you can't trust him. Giant red flag. Like an Alabama-sized red flag. Or Texas, maybe."

"Exactly," Emily said.

"I assume you told him to get lost," Jess said, rummaging through her bag until she unearthed her sunscreen.

"I didn't have a chance," Emily said. "I wasn't thinking straight when I left. Too distracted."

"Distracted by what?"

Emily shrugged. "Jace was there with his real estate agent."

"Jace was on a date with his real estate agent? Does the man have no shame?"

"It looked like they were together. All I could think about was seeing that real estate agent stare at Jace like he was a four-course meal, and she was starving to death."

Jess shook her head. "You really need to go somewhere other than Gulf and Main. Like, absolutely anywhere else. There's a taco truck that parks at the corner of Third and Fourteenth on Thursdays. It serves beer. I'd start there if I were you."

"It just doesn't feel right," Emily said.

"Going somewhere else doesn't feel right? I mean, I know you like your schedules and traditions and all..." Jess paused rubbing the sunscreen on her shoulders. "Wait. What's going on, Em?"

"I told you, Mike—"

"Not with Mike. Screw him. I mean, not literally, not after what he said—" Jess pulled her sunglasses down her nose to look Emily in the eye. "I mean, what's going on with Jason?"

Emily gazed out across the water, pursing her lips. "I have this feeling that Jace has been waiting at Gulf and Main for me every Sunday—pretending to bump into me while I wait for Mike to arrive. He makes small talk, you know? Like, *hello, how are you*. Nothing important. It just felt like he's there waiting to see me."

"Like a stalker? Do we need to call the cops?"

"Well, he knows I meet Mike there every Sunday," Emily said.

"But he was on a *date*, Em. Why would he bring someone to Gulf and Main, knowing you might be there with Mike? Do you think he's trying to make you jealous?"

Emily shook her head. "I don't think that's his style," she said. "Honestly, I don't think it mattered that he was on a date. Even though she was looking at him like she wanted to eat him alive, his attention wasn't on her. It seemed like it was on me."

"Do you think he's interested in getting back together?"

Sighing, Emily said, "I don't know."

"How would you feel about it if he were?"

Emily let the question hang in the air, unanswered.

"You know what he's capable of," Jess added.

"Ripping my heart out?" Emily said, with a bitter laugh. "Yeah, I know all about that one."

"He's capable of *vanishing*, Em," Jess corrected. "He disappeared like a flipping psycho. Who does that? Ask yourself what would happen if he pulled the same shit again."

"Before or after I remove his balls from his body?"

"Harsh," Jess said. "But see? It always comes back to balls."

Emily squinted down the beach. A sandpiper scuttled along the shore. Riders on two horses were slowly walking south along the shoreline within the state park. It looked…lovely.

"Are you going to be mad?" Emily asked quietly, glancing at Jess. "Never mind. You're going to be mad. I can tell."

Her best friend sighed. "You've already decided."

Was Jace really at Gulf and Main so he could say hello? Was he just trying to be her friend, and wasn't interested in anything more? Was she imagining that his attention was on her?

Why was it so difficult to see him on a date with someone else?

She knew the answer to that last question.

And it terrified her.

"I haven't made a decision about Jace," Emily said. "All I know is that he's there when I am, and it can't be a coincidence. And, when I see him there, I want to be sitting next to him, not Mike Malone."

"Gotcha." The sunscreen in Jess's hand closed with a *snap*. "So, as of right now, you've been in town a total of what, like three whole hours? And you've acquired your very own stalker *and* certifiable creep. I'd say that's a new record."

"Thanks for the tally."

"Right. So. First things first, you need to stop seeing the creep. Like, immediately. Or yesterday, whatever comes first."

"I have a date with Mike on Friday night. I'll tell him when I see him."

"You could just text him," Jess said, gesturing towards Emily's cell. "Way quicker."

Emily shook her head. "I'd rather do it in person. He's been nice enough, except for that one comment about the burger."

"And after you tell Mike that he's a giant prick and needs to get lost, you'll talk to Jason and see how it goes. Is that the plan?"

"It's the plan so far."

TWENTY-ONE

Even though it was happy hour, half a dozen tables scattered throughout Gulf and Main were empty, including several spots at the bar. Jason slid into a stool and smiled at Callie as she packed ice into a blender. If she wasn't too busy, maybe he could catch up with her about the tabby cat that had given her a hard time yesterday. Or convince her to adopt one of the remaining pups currently chewing their way through everything in his living room.

Em and her date—Malone, he remembered—were sitting in the corner booth chatting. The guy rubbed Jason the wrong way, but his ex-fiancé seemed to be content enough.

He watched as Em got up and disappeared down the hall to the restroom, adjusting her skirt as she always did. The sight of her still knocked him breathless.

With a wink, Callie slid a margarita toward him on her way to take an order from three women whispering at the other end of the bar. One of them smiled tentatively at him— a tall woman, with blonde hair and striking blue eyes.

Jason looked down at his drink and smiled to himself.

"I'll stop by in a few," Callie said as she drifted by to

deliver three Cosmos to the new arrivals who had seated themselves at a table near Em and her date.

A moment later, there was a crash of broken glass.

He turned to see Callie running into the bartender's area, red-faced, with a dirty, broken glass perched on a tray, looking around frantically for Cass. They spoke, heads bent, whispering furiously. Periodically, Callie glanced over to Em's table, fury contorting her face. Malone was flipping through something on his phone, oblivious.

Jason caught Cass's eye. "What's going on? What's wrong?" he asked.

"Caught that fucker over there spiking a drink," Callie said, nodding in the direction of Em's table. "I saw him do it when I was delivering those Cosmos and Emily was in the bathroom. I bumped into the table on purpose and spilled it before she could get back. Told him I was sorry for being clumsy, and I'd bring him another to replace it."

She turned to Cass. "I needed to take care of it before Emily got back. I didn't want to risk taking the time to come behind the bar and ask what your procedures were for handling those kinds of things. I needed to make sure she didn't drink any, so I spilled it on purpose before she could."

Cass murmured, "It's fine, Callie. Keeping the intended victim safe is more important than anything." She pursed her lips. "Callie, I need you to go into the bathroom—walk calmly—and tell Emily exactly what you saw. I'm going to have a little discussion with today's asshat."

Jason was already off his stool and flying for Em's table before Callie had gotten to the women's room.

The table creaked and tilted a fraction under Jason's weight as he leaned on it, positioning his face level with the son-of-a-bitch sitting there smugly. "Did you think you were going to get away with that?" he whispered dangerously.

Mike glanced up from his phone and smirked. "With what?"

Jason nodded at the wood table, shiny and sticky with a spilled drink intended for Em. "You know exactly what I'm talking about."

"I don't have any idea what you're talking about." Mike took a long swallow of his beer and, locking his eyes with Jason's defiantly, he upended his glass of beer, spilling it all over the table.

"What in the hell are you doing?" Jason said.

Mike laughed. "Fuck you."

"Empty your pockets," Jason growled. "Empty your pockets or I'll empty them for you."

"Again," Mike said, leaning forward, close enough for Jason to feel his breath. "Fuck. You."

Jason launched himself across the table, grabbing Mike's shirt and twisting it to hold him still.

"That's good, everybody," Cass said from behind him.

Jason shoved Mike away, backed up a step, and crossed his arms to keep himself from using his fists. If he did, that fucker might never walk out of Gulf and Main alive.

Mike straightened his shirt and tossed Cass a cocky grin.

"Someone reported that they saw you add something to your date's drink. I'm going to have to ask you to leave," Cass said, crossing her arms in an echo of Jason's.

"Really?" Mike replied.

"Really," she repeated.

Em and Callie emerged from the restroom and made their way over. "What's going on? Mike?" Em asked, horrified, as her eyes swept over the scene.

Ignoring Em's pleading look, Mike said, "Let's go."

"I...I'm going to catch a ride," Em said, planting herself next to Callie.

Mike grunted a reply and slammed his shoulder into Jason's as he stalked out of the bar.

"Callie, leave the table as-is," Cass said before turning to Jason, her eyes fire. "And while I appreciate you stepping in, I can handle anything that happens in my place just fine. You two can stay here for a second and make sure no one else sits down." She pulled her cell phone out of her back pocket. "Excuse me," she barked as she made her way back behind the bar.

After glancing between Jason and Em, Callie scuttled after her.

"Are you okay?" Jason asked.

"I'm not sure. That bartender—the one that works for you—found me in the restroom and told me she saw Mike lace my drink," she said, glancing at the table and shuddering.

"Let's sit for a second," Jason said, pulling out a chair for her. "Maybe don't touch the table, though."

Em nodded. "I can't believe Mike would do that."

"You really can't believe he'd do that?"

Her face fell. "Okay. Part of me isn't surprised," she admitted. "That asshole."

Jason wanted to ask *why on earth would you date that dick*, but he kept his mouth shut.

Cass walked back over with a massive guy in tow.

"This is a friend of mine, Ryan Billings. He's Westshore PD and just happened to be in the neighborhood."

"I was parking my car. I'm supposed to meet some friends here tonight. I'm off duty, but I'm happy to help," he said.

Ryan asked Callie to recount what she'd witnessed, and then asked Jason to describe his interaction with Mike. As the story progressed, Em went from red-faced anger to ghostly pale.

"Can she prosecute?" Jason asked after everything was done.

"Spiking someone's drink is a felony offense in the state of Florida. The problem is," Ryan continued, "from what I understand, the evidence was destroyed."

"Can't you take a sample from the table?" Jason asked.

"He poured his beer out on the same table when you were confronting him, is that correct?" Ryan asked.

Jason nodded. "That's right."

"I've seen cases like this. A sample from the table would not be able to discern which drink had the drug in it originally."

"So that prick can turn around and accuse Em of spiking *his* drink?" Jason said, flabbergasted.

"I've seen it go that way." Ryan shifted on his feet. "Look, I'm not here in any official capacity. But I suspect that since Ms. Driscoll did not consume any of the beverage, there would be little value in pursuing it further."

"Just Emily, please, officer," Em said.

Ryan nodded.

"Other than another woman might be spared a lifetime of trauma next time he pulls this bullshit," Cass cut in, staring levelly at the cop.

"I don't disagree, Cass. But there's not much I can do, I'm afraid," he said. It didn't look like Ryan liked what he was saying any more than they did. "You're welcome to call the station, have someone head over, and give them your statement," he continued. "It's up to you."

Em shook her head. "I…" She swallowed. "I think I just want to go home."

"I'll be around if you change your mind or have further questions," Ryan said before nodding and making his way across the bar.

"All is not lost," Cass said after a long breath. "I'll make a few calls. Some of the other bar owners around town might be interested to know what happened here tonight."

TWENTY-TWO

The ride from Gulf and Main to her townhouse felt endless.

The silence didn't help.

Emily couldn't find the right words to say anyway.

What do you say to an ex-fiancé driving you home after your date tried to drug you? Was it *thanks for showing up to rescue me tonight?* Or, *if you had shown up at our wedding, you wouldn't have needed to show up tonight to rescue me?*

After Ryan, Cass, and Callie went back to, well, whatever they'd been doing while Mike Malone laced her drink, Jace had quietly led her out of the bar to his Jeep.

She mumbled vague directions and spent the rest of the time watching buildings flit by, illuminated by the streetlights, trying to think of a way to thank him.

Was her life always going to be one disaster after another?

"Here," she murmured, and Jace pulled the Jeep into her driveway.

"I'm going to stay here in the car for a while, just to make sure you're safe," he said quietly. "If that's okay with you."

She nodded, and by the time she'd closed the door and locked herself inside, he'd already cut the engine.

The next morning, Emily drove to her mom's cottage, needing the beach, saltwater, and her mom's comforting presence to cleanse her thoughts and her soul. She hadn't heard Jace's car drive away last night but based on how long it took her to get to sleep, she figured he hadn't left until well past three in the morning.

She *still* wasn't sure how to feel about it. How do you process your ex-fiancé guarding you from some nut-job from high school who tried to drug you?

It was like living in *Twilight Zone, Westshore Beach Edition.*

When Emily arrived at the cottage, her mom gave her one look then smiled gently, almost knowingly. Thankfully, her mom knew better than to ask for details.

Emily settled on the deck as the waves rumbled and the breeze picked up. A storm was on its way. She pulled out her cell and pulled up the last text she got from Jace—one she had left unanswered. Instead of answering it, she typed:

I have a problem

Jace's reply came within a minute.

How can I help?

you know how much I like routine

She could feel Jace smiling as he typed his reply.

I happen to remember that

I'm used to going to G&M for brunch every Sunday

I'll wait for you there

"Em," her mom called through the open kitchen window. "I forgot to tell you. I'm getting new neighbors. Someone bought the cottage next door. It wasn't even listed for a week before it was sold."

"Maybe a nice firefighter will move in," Emily called back. "And maybe he'll like goat yoga and purple tie-dye."

Her mom appeared at the screen door, eyebrow raised, playful smile lighting her face. "Then you'll have to help me start a couple of fires around here."

All week, Emily could barely think of anything but seeing Jace at Gulf and Main the following weekend.

Sunday morning, Emily managed to keep herself from driving to the pub the moment she awoke. It would be futile anyway—Jace always used to slip in the moment before he was technically late.

Well, she thought, *it was either wait for Jace here at home, pacing my bedroom and second-guessing my choice in footwear, or wait at the pub, where I could sit and sip a more-than-welcome coffee.*

Better the bar than home, she supposed.

As she pulled into a parking space in front of Gulf and Main precisely at 12:30 p.m., she noticed a deep red Jeep swing into the opposite side of the lot.

Jace.

Also ridiculously early.

Strange.

"Hey, you," he called as he got out of his Jeep and sauntered toward her car.

Emily couldn't help but smile. He'd dressed in jeans and a white button-down rolled halfway up to his elbows, the fabric of the shirt straining against his massive biceps and forearms.

How on earth did he manage to look like he spent hours at the gym when he was very likely at his veterinary clinic all day?

And how in the hell is a man who looks like that still single?

She swallowed. Those arms were the very definition of *arm porn.*

She dragged her stare from his arms to his chiseled jaw, and blushing, she met his eye.

Jace looked at her curiously. "You okay?"

"Absolutely," she said, heading for the door. "Just surprised to see you here this early."

He gave her an apologetic smile. "I know you value being punctual. I used to push that envelope a lot—arrive thirty seconds before the movie started, for instance. I know how much that used to drive you crazy," he said. "I guess I'm trying to do better. Make up for it, if you let me."

Emily gave him a sidelong glance as they walked inside.

Jace led her to a table with a hand-written reserved sign sitting at its center and pulled out a chair.

"I didn't even know they reserved tables here," she said.

"I'm not sure they do either," he said with a sly smile. "But the owner seems to think she owes me a favor or two."

After they ordered drinks and brunch, Jace told her about the Lab and puppies he was fostering.

"I have five puppies and the mother, who I've named Molly," he said. "One of the puppies—a female—is very attached to the mom. I'm hoping that whoever adopts the little guy is willing to come visit a lot."

"I'm sure you're vetting the potential owners as if they

were applying for a top-secret government contract," Emily said.

He chuckled. "Let's just say it helps if you know me already."

Brunch was just as delicious as it was every Sunday. They fell into easy conversation, and eventually Emily realized that they were the only ones left in the pub.

"I guess we should go," she said, noticing the empty seats and Cass wiping the bar.

Jace held the front door open for her and followed her to her car.

"You know, I'd like to see your new place sometime," Emily said.

Jace's staggeringly blue eyes lit up. "Really?"

"Yeah. Why not?" Emily said. "You have to introduce me to the puppies."

"Okay," he said. "How about next Sunday afternoon after brunch? You can follow me over."

She hesitated. "Well, I guess I'm open."

"Then I'll see you here next week at 1."

Next Sunday's brunch was much the same—Emily found that time slipped away when she was talking to Jace—and there were moments when she forgot that the man sitting next to her was the same man that was responsible for shredding her heart and very nearly ruining her life.

After brunch, Emily followed Jace's maroon Jeep through Westshore to his new house. After a minute he turned down Gulf Boulevard toward the beach.

This is the way to mom's cottage.

He turned onto Eighteenth Street.

Wait, this is her street. And up ahead is her place.

He pulled into the driveway next door to her mom's house, next to the real estate sign that now flaunted the word *SOLD* diagonally across the relator's information in bright white letters on a red background.

This has to be some sort of cosmic joke. This is a joke, right?

Driving past Jace's cottage, Emily pulled into her mom's driveway and shifted her car into park, leaving the engine running. With a smile, he got out of his Jeep, slamming the door behind him. "Hey, do you know the people that live—"

"My mom. My mom lives here," she sputtered.

A moment ago, she could decide when and if and how long she'd see Jace. Every Sunday, for instance, for a couple of hours. And that was it. She could keep him confined to a little box, one she took out whenever she decided to, one she could put away when things got too familiar.

When they got too close.

Suddenly, it was as if Jace was back, and she had no say in it.

Everything was spinning out of her control.

Emily swallowed. "Look. I...I need to go," she said, slammed her car into reverse, and sped away.

TWENTY-THREE

"**I** can't believe it," Emily said. "First, he moves to Westshore Beach. Now, he lives right next to Mom."

From behind her book, her best friend grunted a reply without bothering to look up.

"That must be one heck of a good book," Emily groused.

It was Monday, and Emily and Jess were rooted in their usual spot at South Cove Beach to watch the volleyball game. Jace's cousin, Tyler, was playing today, and, strangely, Jess was reading a book instead of expressing her usual enthusiasm for tan muscles, spikes, and dives.

Tyler chose that moment to jog over to them, volleyball in hand. He bent to kiss the top of Jess's hair, winking at Emily. Jess beamed at him, abandoning her book for the moment.

"I mean, this is utterly ridiculous," Emily continued. "Right next door? *Come. On.* How am I going to go for a jog down the beach if he lives right there?"

"The universe is conspiring to get you two together again," Tyler said as he continued to stare at Jess.

Emily rolled her eyes. "They're waiting for you," she said,

pointing at the volleyball court behind him.

Tyler chuckled, brushed a kiss across Jess's cheek, and jogged away.

Emily wasn't anywhere near finished. "You know how close those cottages are? When he's on his deck, you can talk to him from Mom's! Now every time I'm there, he'll be within earshot!"

"There's no way he could have known, Em," Jess said levelly. "What are you afraid of?"

It was a great question. Why was she so upset?

She pictured Jace on his deck. His hair stirring in the gentle, early-morning gulf breeze. Coffee at his lips. An easy smile. And behind him, the slider opening and a woman's voice calling—

Shaking the image out of her mind, Emily sighed. "I hate this."

"Do you?" Jess met her eye. "I mean…maybe it's a good thing. You'll get even more used to seeing him and it won't be a big deal any longer. You know, get back on the pony right away."

Tyler spiked a serve, scoring a point, and signaled for a time out to remove his indecently tight t-shirt. Emily sighed again. Tyler and Jace shared the same body type: chests thick with muscle, narrow waists, broad shoulders. Sharp jawlines. Bright blue eyes that whispered of a wicked sense of humor and a teasing bedroom.

She missed the feel of Jace, the weight of him, the smell of him...*dammit.*

Tyler leapt up to set a ball, his arms stretched upward. Emily blinked at his upper arm.

"Hey, does Tyler have a tattoo?" she said.

"Yeah," Jess mumbled from behind her book. "Left arm. Underside."

Squinting at Jace's cousin as he spiked the ball again, Emily said, "It looks good."

Finally, Jess poked her head out of her book to glance over at the volleyball game. Nodding, she said, "Sure does."

Maybe Jess was right—maybe all she needed was time to get used to the idea that Jace was now living next to her mom. She didn't want to cancel her brunch date with Jace, she told herself, just postpone it. She'd be ready by next Sunday. One hundred percent ready by then. Absolutely.

Fishing her cell out of her bag, she found Jace in her contacts and typed:

Can we postpone our brunch until next week?

Her phone buzzed almost immediately. Somehow a gang of butterflies in her stomach decided it was time to celebrate. She told the butterflies to shut up.

Sure. Looking forward to seeing you then.

Emily dropped down on one of her mom's deck chairs, damp with dew, and bent to tie her running shoes, sighing gratefully.

No running away for this girl anymore, thank-you-very-much. Just jogs up and down the beach.

Her best friend had encouraged her to resume her exercise routine—*it'll set you right as snowflakes,* Jess had said when she dropped off Emily after they'd spent the afternoon watching Tyler and the other guys play. *It'd be good for you.*

Jess was right. It had been far too long since Emily had done anything but sit, whether it was at a bar or at the beach.

So, Emily had set her alarm for five a.m. the next

morning and drove through the wakening sky to her mom's cottage, intending to go for a jog before the day became too stifling. Snaggles had wanted to come, but based on his age, the cast on his still-recovering leg, and his tendency to dart away when off-leash, she decided to leave him at home.

I'm going for a run, she reminded herself, as she stretched. *Not running away. Right.*

At the sound of a screen door opening, she glanced over to Jace's cottage.

Jace squinted at the shore, the morning's first cup of coffee in hand. The aroma of toasted hazelnuts mingled with the salty air. Molly and two of the pups milled around his feet, sniffing, wagging, and exploring.

Her mom chose that moment to join Emily on the deck.

Turning at the sound of her mom's screen door closing, Jason nodded, bringing the cup to his lips. "Morning, Mrs. Lanson. Morning, Em."

Board shorts hung low on his hips.

Stubble accented his sharp jaw.

Perfectly tumbled hair as if he'd just—

Well, *shit.*

Damn the man to hell, he'd no right to look that good.

He looked stronger and more muscled than he ever had, as if his job depended on pushups, pullups, and sit-ups rather than a stethoscope and a gentle touch. Wide shoulders narrowed impressively into the sharp V of his waist, his abs looking harder than they had a right to. A distinctive notch angled away from his hip and pointed downward toward—

Emily realized she was staring. She felt her face flush and turned away.

Stop it, Emily.

Jace seemed not to notice. Well, he was probably used to it. Who wouldn't stare at him?

Memories forced their way to the front of her mind—
Jace was always up early after a late night of tangled sheets
and whispered sighs. He liked to rise and make breakfast. Put
on a pot of coffee.

And kiss me awake.

Often, they would eat in bed, and soon after, return to
more tangled sheets, more sighs.

She blinked, her heart bruising with the memory.

What would she do if someone followed him out?

Thankfully, Jace seemed to be alone.

Well, not *quite* alone. The puppies were busy investigating
the deck as if they were looking for hidden treasures.

A steaming coffee mug in hand, he squinted at the shore
then smiled down at the dogs. He brought the cup to his lips,
and she could almost imagine his grateful sigh, the one that
reminded her of honey. And chocolate.

Stop it, Emily, she told herself. *Just stop.*

There was no way she should be thinking of what his
sighs sounded like. Not when his hair was messy and the man
apparently couldn't find a shirt to save his life, even though
the damp air was cool enough to make her shiver.

The puppies bustled around, rooting into all the edges as
if he'd been training them for search and rescue. One nosed
around in a plant pot, coming up with dirt covering his little
black wet nose.

Emily bent to stretch her hamstrings. Molly watched Jace
expectantly until Emily padded out onto the cold sand. The
Lab let out a single bark, as she paced behind the baby gate
installed across the stairs to keep the puppies from accessing
the beach.

"Looks like someone wants to go with you," Jace called.

Emily spoke before she thought it through. "Is that
okay?" she called back. "I'd love some company."

Nodding again, Jace managed to let Molly out without any of the puppies escaping. "Molly's great off-leash," he said as the dog rushed toward her, eyes alight and mouth stretched in a goofy dog smile.

"I won't be long," Emily said. "I haven't run in a while so I'm not going far."

The Lab looked ready to burst with excitement—she tried her best to sit at Emily's feet, tail thumping enthusiastically. But every time Emily moved a fraction, the dog spun in a circle, eager to go.

"Ready?" Emily asked.

They flew down the beach side by side, Molly's tongue lolling to the side and ears flopping as she bounded alongside Emily down the empty beach.

When she returned with Molly at her side, both happily out of breath, Jace waved the dog inside the gate, and that was that.

TWENTY-FOUR

Emily didn't always see Jace from her mom's deck in the early mornings before her daily run along Westshore beach. If he were home, Molly would race back and forth along the baby gate until Jace let her out. Together, Emily and the black Lab would fly down the sand, her ponytail bobbing in time with the chilly morning air filling her lungs.

There were mornings when it looked like Jace wasn't home—Emily tried her best not to think about those mornings, but she couldn't stop wondering why he wasn't there. Hadn't he come home the night before? Was he still in bed? Was someone else in bed with him, inside?

Well, if he was entertaining someone on those nights—or mornings—there had never been another car in the driveway. Or an Uber stopping at the cottage.

She'd never know, and it was eating her up inside.

She needed to stop. Speculating wouldn't help anyone, especially her.

This particular morning, however, Jace was home.

"Looks like someone thinks they are going jogging with you again," he said, glancing down at Molly as she paced around the deck, tongue lolling. "Any time you'd like to take her, just let me know."

"She's welcome to come, as always," Emily called back.

Jace opened the gate at the top of the stairs and Molly galloped down, sand flying, all happy-dog energy. Emily laughed.

Her ex-fiancé strolled over, black coffee in hand.

"Thanks," Emily said as she stretched her muscles awake. Molly ran in circles, eager to go.

"You know I'm not much of a runner," Jace said. "I'm thankful when you take her with you. Some mornings I need to get to the clinic by five to check on a patient, so I'm not even here," he said.

So that explained it.

She hated that his words made her feel better.

She hated that he told her.

She hated that he *felt the need* to tell her.

"I can give you the garage code so you can take her jogging with you when I'm not home, if you want," he continued.

Garage code?

Emily tried to say something but failed.

"Well, think about it," he continued. "You're welcome to it. Might be faster than me finding time to get a key made."

A key? What?

Emily blinked and continued to warm up. A key to his place? Does that mean he's not worried about me walking in on—

"I didn't know you liked running on the beach," Jace said.

She blinked away the surprise of his offer and shrugged. "I didn't know it either. Not until I tried it."

Jace nodded and turned back to his cottage. "Have fun," he said over his shoulder.

A pang of loss hit her in the chest as he turned away.

She swallowed and tried to focus on finishing her stretches.

Emily had been running every day for a week now, and today—after reading an article she'd happened upon online—she'd decided to run barefoot for the first time. As Molly sprinted in circles, Emily untied her running shoes and abandoned them on the stairs to her mom's deck.

The cool sand felt fabulous between her toes.

Smiling, she took off, loping south past her mom's cottage, down along the shoreline with Molly at her side. To her right, the dense foliage of the state park sang with cicadas and frogs, waking with the day. The air was crisp and perfect, the sun had just broken over the horizon, the sound of the gulls echoing happily with the gently breaking waves.

Step-stride, step-stride, step-stride.

It was much more demanding to run barefoot. And much more fun.

Five minutes into the run, her foot struck something sickeningly sharp. A broken shell? Collapsing on the sand with a yelp, she glanced at the bottom of her foot—and gasped.

It was bleeding. Badly.

Oh no, no, no—

Her stomach roiled. Her hands shook.

Molly plopped down beside her, breathing hard, as Emily glanced up and down the beach. No one was in sight.

What on earth made her leave her cell in her car this morning?

She couldn't—or maybe *shouldn't*—put weight on her foot. How was she going to get back?

"Molly, go get Jace," she said as earnestly as she could to the dog. Molly cocked her head to the side.

Who do I think I'm talking to? Molly's not a curiously smart collie with her own television show.

Emily took a deep breath. There was no way the dog would understand, but she tried pointing in the direction of Jace's cottage anyway. "Go on, girl. Go."

The Lab blinked once and took off at a run.

Had Molly chosen that moment to run away? Would Jace notice that she hadn't come back, but Molly had?

Her foot throbbed. She lay on the sand as her eyes pricked with tears.

What if Jace didn't come? How would she get back? Would she have to crawl back to her mom's house? Or wait for the state park to open and someone to wander by, then ask them to call for help?

Not more than a couple of minutes later, a figure of a man appeared in the distance down the beach, headed in her direction.

Jace.

And he was *running.*

If her foot didn't make her want to weep, she would have laughed. Even as it was, she let out a little chuckle through her pain: Jace was dashing toward her as if his shorts were on fire, following one determined Labrador retriever.

Molly made it to her first and laid down at her side. "Thank you, Molly," she whispered. "Good girl."

"You okay, Em?" Jace said, kneeling in the sand beside her.

"I cut my heel…" She let the words trail off, desperately forcing down the need to cry.

"Let me see," he said, taking her foot in his hands. "It's a decent laceration. Looks like you stepped on glass."

"You sound like a doctor," she said, trying to distract herself and keep the conversation light as the fiery pain in her foot pulsed with every heartbeat.

"Well, I have stayed at a Holiday Inn Express," he quipped. "And I have a good reference in the form of a little dog with crooked teeth that likes to chase cars."

"The best kind," she said, grimacing.

Glancing down the beach toward his cottage, Jace continued, "I'm going to help you stand. Keep your weight on the other leg. Once you're standing, I'm going to pick you up and carry you back. Is that okay?"

She nodded. A tear leaked out of her eye and down her cheek.

Holding out his hand, he helped her rise and then lifted her easily, supporting her weight with one arm under her knees. Emily let her head fall against his chest.

She'd never guessed she'd ever be this close to Jace again.

The smell of him flooded her lungs and made her head spin, driving out any thought of her injury.

He smelled of coffee and pine trees and fresh-cut grass.

And something that was uniquely *him*.

Jace—

Something profound wrenched inside her: the tough, ugly scar of *you left me*, twisted and pulled by the supple skin of *what if*.

She pushed it aside.

Each step he took sent a jolt of pain screaming up her leg.

I refuse to cry, she thought. Besides, Jace is here. *He'll know exactly what to do.*

Once they reached his cottage, Emily managed to stand on her right foot and stay upright—grasping the deck's wooden handrail as if her life depended on it—while he unlocked the baby gate and quickly herded the puppies into the house. A door closed—maybe a bedroom—and Jace reappeared, a towel in hand.

He offered her a soft smile. "Let's get you to the bathroom," Jace said, and swooped her up again, lifting her as if she weighed nothing.

Jace carried her down a short hallway—swiveling to the side so her foot wouldn't hit the wall—and into a tiny bathroom covered in cheery yellow paint. Ever so gently, he placed her on the counter next to the sink and backed away, as if he wasn't sure exactly how to let her go.

Blood had run down his leg. At the sight of it, she felt her face drain of color.

"Thanks," she said softly, tears welling in her eyes.

"No problem," he said softly, handing her a tissue.

"I don't want to look. I don't have to look, do I?"

"No, you don't have to look, Em."

Jace ran the cold water and guided her foot underneath the stream. She gasped.

When he finished examining it, his face was somber. "It's not too bad, but it looks like you might need stitches. Maybe three, but probably just two."

I'll have to go to the emergency room and I'll—

Even in her head, she couldn't get herself to complete the sentence.

Her palms were sticky with sweat.

Her stomach heaved.

Her fingers started to shake.

Gritting her teeth, Emily balled her hands into fists and fought the tremors as best she could.

"Let me take you to a walk-in clinic," Jace said evenly. "The closest one is at Main and Thirtieth but I'm not sure how early it's open on Sundays. It might not be open at all. If it's closed, we can head over to the ER."

Dread clawed at her chest, momentarily crowding out the pain. The echo-y corridors, the smell of alcohol, the hum and beep of monitors, the murmurs of doctors from down the hallway—

"It's no problem, Em. It's probably just one stitch," he said. "Maybe two. Easy and fast, I promise. I'll stay with you, if you want."

Panic rose like a tide, threatening to drown her. She felt herself crawling away into a ball.

If you go to the emergency room, you never leave.

Emily swallowed, her foot throbbing. "Don't you—can't you—I mean, you're a vet, so you can do stitches. Can't you do it?"

"Not legally." Jace stood silently for a moment, his head cocked to the side as if he were considering something. "But I know what going to a clinic or the ER would be like for you, and I don't want to put you through that. So, yeah, I can do a suture. Are you sure you want me to do it?"

"Please," she whispered. "You know I can't go to either place. Especially the hospital. I...I don't...I can't..." Terror glued the rest of the words in her throat.

"I can clean the wound and put a stitch in, but I don't have anything to numb it or anything for the pain," he said levelly.

"I understand," she said. "It's okay. I'd still rather you do it."

Jace nodded grimly. "I'll be back in a minute."

She took a deep breath. It was going to be okay. Jace would help her. She didn't need to go...*there.*

He returned with a large plastic bottle, placed it on the counter next to her, and pulled on a pair of latex gloves. "This ugly brown stuff is an antiseptic," he said, pointing at the bottle. "It won't sting, I promise."

"So many promises in one day," Emily managed, trying for a hint of a smile. "First, you said this was going to be fast and easy. Now, you're saying this won't sting. I have no idea what you're going to promise next."

"I'm not used to having a conversation with my patients and having them respond," he said with his own suggestion of a smile. "It's a little unnerving."

"Says the man who is about to sew me back together. Shouldn't I be the one who's unnerved?"

"Ready?"

Nodding, Emily drew a sharp breath as he cleaned the cut.

"What made you leave your running shoes behind?" Jace asked as he worked.

"I did some research," Em said, wincing. "Running barefoot on the sand forces small stabilizer muscles to work, improves balance, burns more calories, and allows for a more optimal foot strike."

"Sounds impressive."

"Not so much after you land on glass and need to be rescued by your ex."

He huffed a laugh and continued to work.

"Damn tourists," he said, producing a long shard of glass in his tweezers for her to examine before discarding it on a tissue.

"Damn tourists," she echoed, shuddering.

"You're going to need to stay perfectly still. Florida has a Good Samaritan Law, but I still don't want to have to explain this in court."

She breathed a nervous laugh.

When he was finished, Jace covered the wound with a bandage and cleaned up.

"Even though it's your left foot, I'm guessing you're not going to want to drive home quite yet. I don't have to be anywhere until this afternoon. How about we move over to the couch for a little while?"

"Sure."

Jace wrapped his arm around her waist to support her down the hall; they passed a second bedroom that she hadn't noticed on the way in, filled with free weights, a rowing machine, and a collection of other gym equipment that she couldn't quite see. In the cozy living room, a fat leather couch took up most of the space, along with a television, and another overstuffed chair. She settled on the couch and gingerly placed her left foot up on the coffee table.

"You choose," he said, handing her the television remote and disappearing into the kitchen. He returned with two coffee mugs and offered her one, settling on the chair next to the couch.

Molly curled up at Emily's right foot, and five sleepy puppies waddled in, nosing their way in beside their mother.

"They're adorable," Emily said.

"Molly was a stray," Jace said. "She had the puppies underneath someone's deck over on Twenty-seventh Street. The shelter didn't have room and, since the homeowners didn't want to call animal control, they called me."

She blinked in surprise. "You went and got them?"

"They needed help."

"You lucked out. Molly is amazing," Emily said.

"I foster dogs from my clinic every once in a while, so it was no problem." He smiled, his eyes sparkling. "It's partially why I wanted to move to a bigger place," he said. "My condo was tiny."

"Smaller than this?"

"Yeah, if you can believe it. I named the big guy Flint," Jace continued, pointing at a fat, round puppy currently asleep with his back legs stretched out behind him. "The others are Sadie, Gracie, Zoey, and Milo," he said. "At least, that's what I'm calling them."

"Do you have homes for all of them?"

"I'm working on it. One of my vet techs—Mel—is going to take Milo," he said with a wistful smile at the tiny black puppy who was sniffing Emily's uninjured foot. "And I'm going to keep Molly, of course."

"She's a great dog," Emily said. "When I stepped on the glass, she sat down next to me, as if she knew I was in pain, and it would be difficult for me to get back. When I told her to go get you, I swore she looked at me as if she understood what I was saying. She knew exactly where to go and what to do."

"She was barking up a storm at the gate. I opened it to let her back in and she barked and took off down the beach. When I realized you hadn't come back with her—"

Her belly growled, loud enough to interrupt Jace. Her face heated. "Sorry. I never eat before I run—I eat with Mom after I get back."

"I'll make us something," he said, standing up.

"You don't need to do that. I've put you through enough already this morning. It's okay. Really."

"I'm hungry myself. It's no problem to make a little more."

Jace disappeared into the kitchen.

"Still like pancakes?" he called. "I can easily make them vegan."

"Uh…yeah. Sure. That'd be great."

The clink of a metal frying pan on a stovetop and the sound of a refrigerator door opening had Emily wishing she could get up and watch. The smell of warm maple syrup made her belly rumble even more.

"Would it be okay if I used your phone?" Emily called.

"Turning me in for the stitches already, huh? That was

fast," he said from the kitchen.

"I need to text my mom, so she isn't wondering where I disappeared to."

Jace brought her his cell and returned to the kitchen. As she held it in her hand, her throat tightened. *Please*, she thought, *don't let anyone text him right now. Don't let me see anything that would make today hurt even more.*

Emily sent a quick text to her mom, and her mom acknowledged it with a tie-dye thumbs-up emoji. Doing her best not to disturb the puppies, she reached as far as she could away from her and laid the phone face down.

Jace appeared with a plate of pancakes, a glass of orange juice, and a sheepish smile.

Apparently, Jason Williams, DVM had learned to cook since she'd known him last.

Apparently, he'd learned a lot of things.

Dare she hope that he'd learned how to stay?

TWENTY-FIVE

Jason slid into his favorite barstool at Gulf and Main and winked at Callie from across the bar. The feelings he'd long suppressed for Em were beginning to take over his life. Every moment of every day they'd wiggle in from his subconscious, keeping him up at night. It was past time for him to get some advice.

Tyler was out of the country again—damn inconvenient timing, truly—but considering that Callie was a self-proclaimed expert in matters of the heart, he bet that she'd know exactly what he should do.

"Well, look who's here," she said with one of her trademark stunning smiles. "What can I do you for, Boss?"

"Just an ice water for now, Callie."

"Meeting somebody? Want me to grab the corner booth for you?" she asked as she filled a glass and set it in front of him.

"Nope. I came to see you."

"I'm honored." She leaned forward on the bar and, if anything, smiled more widely. "Tell me why you're really here in the middle of a Saturday afternoon all by yourself."

Jason huffed a laugh. "I need some advice."

"I'm listening."

He took a deep breath and let it out slowly. "Em and I…"

"Obviously," she said after he trailed off. Her eyes twinkled. "You two are meant to be together. I already mentioned that."

"You did."

"What else?" Callie asked. "Wait—" She put her hand up as if stopping a car, looked up to the ceiling as if it would spill secrets, and said nothing for a moment. Then: "So *you're* the asshole that hurt her."

Of course. There was no hiding anything from Callie, Oracle and Acute Observer of All.

Jason barked a laugh. "Don't hold back, Callie."

"I just call 'em as I see 'em, Boss." She leaned back, hands on hips. "I could never figure out why she went out with that Mike guy. Now it all makes sense."

"How so?"

"It's a strange thing, you see. Sometimes people that have been hurt are so afraid they'll get hurt again, they subconsciously choose to date people that aren't the right match, the right fit. It keeps them from getting too seriously attached, and therefore keeps them from getting hurt again."

"That sounds like a load of crap, if you ask me."

"I didn't ask you, now did I? Mind you, I'm not claiming any psychology degrees or even anything close. Seems reasonable, though." She shrugged. "I'm sure there's a part of Emily that was trying to move on, too, and Mike just happened to be around."

"Or she was trying to make me jealous."

"Nah. Not her deal," Callie said.

"Fair enough," Jason conceded.

Acute Observer, indeed.

"Well?" she prodded.

"Em and I…have a bit of…history."

"What you're trying to say is that you're the one who blew it. I'm pretty sure we just covered this when I said that you were the one that hurt her."

Jason grunted a reply and took a sip of his ice water.

Callie grabbed premixed a margarita in a plastic cup and set it in front of him. "I'm gonna need a bit more info than that."

Jason cleared his throat and traced the rim of the margarita with his finger, spilling lumps of salt onto the bar. "I walked out on her."

Callie's eyes widened slightly. She waited, staring at him relentlessly.

"More specifically, I ghosted her three days before we were supposed to get married."

She whistled under her breath. "Damn."

Sighing, he continued, "I was supposed to meet her in Cancún for our wedding. When she flew to Mexico, I quit my job, moved out of my apartment, and changed my number. That was a little more than eight years ago. I didn't see her or talk to her until I bumped into her in Westshore, a couple months ago."

Callie shook her head. "Seriously?"

"Yeah," he said, abandoning the ice water and taking a long swallow of the margarita.

"Damn," she said again.

They stared at each other for a minute.

"I have to say, that's pretty fucking low. Like really fucking low. And I don't use the f-word all that often, but I think this situation merits it," she said.

"Probably," he murmured.

"I'm surprised she even speaks to you."

"Right." Jason downed the rest of his drink.

"Why'd you do it?" she asked, replacing his empty cup with a fresh one.

Jason pursed his lips. "Good question."

Callie stood there, hands on hips once more, and waited.

"It's a good question—and I don't have a good answer." He sighed again, dragging his fingers through his hair. "I had a bit of a freak-out. I can't blame it on anything else. And I can't explain it. Not to anyone's satisfaction. Even mine."

"That's asinine, Boss."

"Yup." He took a gulp of the new margarita.

Callie cocked her head and said nothing for a long while. Then: "Are you still scared enough to run?"

"I'm more scared that I'll never get her back."

She hummed a reply.

"What am I supposed to do?" he said.

"Let me think," Callie murmured. Grabbing a white linen towel from a cabinet to her left, she started polishing rings off the bar.

"I'm royally fucked, aren't I?" Jason said.

"You might be."

Three guys came in the front door and settled down at the other end of the bar. With a wink, Callie vanished to take their orders.

"One thing's for certain, Boss," she said when she returned from serving beer to the newcomers. "You're going to have to show up, no matter where, no matter when. If you say you're going to be somewhere, or do something, you *must* follow through. There can't ever be an excuse. You can't ever be late, and never, ever, a no-show."

"Done," he said.

"Patience, first, though," Callie said. "You need to go

slowly. It's going to take a while for Emily to trust you."

"Makes sense."

"And woo her. I mean it, Boss. Whatever she likes—over the top. Watch the sunset. Cook her favorite dinners, take her to her favorite restaurants. Become the most frequent customer of that florist that opened up two doors down from here. Pretend you're the good guy in a Hallmark movie. Make sure she feels like no one else could even come close. Tell her that she's the first thing you think of when you wake up in the morning and the last thing you think of when you're about to fall asleep, and the only thing you think about in all the moments in between. You know, do all the things that I know you're capable of."

"Okay."

She flicked open a clean folded white linen towel and began to polish a wine glass. "Just prepare yourself in case it doesn't work."

"I need to talk to you, Mom," Emily said, leaning back on the counter across from her mom, whose attention was on a bunch of flowers she was freeing from a clear, plastic sleeve.

"Well, I suppose that's why you're here," her mom said with a warm smile as she cut the ends off sunflower stems before placing them in a glass vase, one by one.

"Those are beautiful, by the way."

"They are, aren't they? A new florist opened on Seventeenth Avenue—Danny's Lions. You know, like 'dande-lions'? Cute name, don't you think?"

"I do," Emily said.

Her mom took a step back from the counter, tilting her head to the side to examine the arrangement critically, then adjusted one of the sunflowers to the left. Without turning to

Emily, she said, "It's okay."

"What's okay?" Emily asked, baffled.

"What you're about to tell me." Her mom pushed open the screen door to the deck with her shoulder and placed the vase in the center of the wrought iron table.

After a deep breath, Emily followed, the screen door slamming shut behind her. "How do you know that it'll be okay?" she asked.

Her mom smiled. "I think it will be." She wiggled another stem until the face of the flower swiveled slightly to the right.

Emily walked to the railing, her eyes on the surf. "*I'm* not even sure it's okay."

"It is," her mom said gently, abandoning the sunflowers to walk across the deck and stand alongside her.

"I still love him. I don't think I ever stopped." Emily felt the truth of the words as they tumbled from her lips. Speaking them aloud seemed to change everything all at once.

Her mom nodded and leaned heavily on the railing.

"Do you think it's stupid of me to try?"

Raising an eyebrow, her mom said, "Stupid? I don't know. Unwise? Maybe." She put her arm around Emily and drew her close. "Is it ever stupid to give love a second chance?"

"I don't know, Mom."

"Only you can make that decision, Em," her mom said. "Just know I'm here, and whatever happens, I'm still here. I'll always be here."

Her mom squeezed her and disappeared inside the cottage as Emily kept her eyes on the gulf stretching out before her. If she squinted hard enough, she could almost imagine she could see Cancún on the other side.

Jason wandered onto his deck, Molly and the puppies milling around his feet. Em and her mom were out on the deck next door, their eyes on the setting sun.

He waved a hello. "Walk down the beach?" Jason called.

Em and her mom glanced at each other. Her mom shook her head and said something to her daughter that he couldn't hear.

"Okay," Em called back, and descended the deck's wooden steps to wait for him.

They walked in silence, meandering down the beach and avoiding the gentle waves lapping over the sand. Coquinas bobbed up, retreating downward each time the tide withdrew.

The sun painted the clouds a soft peach.

People started to arrive to watch the sunset. Tourists, mainly, filtering in from the beach access points in their shorts and shirts, some with shoes in hand, squinting toward the sinking sun. Most stayed near the steps to the parking areas, only there for a short stop on their way to dinner or an evening's adventures.

A couple emerged from the crowd to make their way closer to the shoreline. The woman's skin was pink from the day's sun, and her sandals dangled from one hand. With her other, she held onto her husband, stealing glances at him as they wandered toward the water. Her husband seemed content, as if he had everything he wanted or could ever want right there beside him.

That man had never messed up as badly as Jason had.

A flare of anguish pulled at him. Would he ever be free of the guilt for what he'd done to Em? To their relationship? To their lives?

The waves grew stronger, and Em moved around him to the beach side to keep her sneakers from getting wet, her hand accidentally brushing his.

A jolt of recognition—of longing—sang through him.

"You and I...we loved each other once." The words slipped out before he realized he'd said them.

Em didn't respond for a moment. Then: "We did."

Glancing down the shore to the couple walking hand in hand, he said, "I still remember what it was like when you were mine. I remember what it was to be in love with you. My heart—my soul—remembers."

For a moment, they watched the waves in the fading light and the sandpipers darting along the water's edge, then turned as one to continue down the beach.

Em was silent. What was she feeling? Surely if she weren't interested in being near him, she wouldn't have agreed to come?

They kept walking.

The sun set, the light bathing the sand in purple.

By mutual, silent agreement, they turned around in the deepening dark, a lone seagull's cries accompanying their footfall.

The sight of his cottage came far too quickly.

The sounds of Em's mom moving around her kitchen drifted out her open window with the buttery light.

"Sit on the deck with me?" Jason said, doing his best to keep the desperation out of his voice.

"Sure," she said softly.

Once more, he brushed her hand as they climbed the four steps up to his deck. He settled on the swing and waited.

Eyes luminous in the darkness, Em stood as if she were deliberating something particularly difficult. A moment later, in one fluid motion, she sank into the swing next to him, curling into his arms.

He thought he might weep.

She leaned her head against him, and he snaked his arm

around her shoulders. She snuggled in closer.

"What are we doing, Jace?"

"We're sitting on my deck."

"Is that all?"

The waves broke along the shoreline, scattering the seagulls scouring the sand for food.

"We're doing what we used to do," he said into the gathering dark. "Are you afraid?"

"I'm terrified."

Jason brushed her hair back behind her shoulder. Her eyes fluttered shut.

"I decided something. I don't want to be your friend, Em."

She opened her eyes and pulled away. "You don't?"

"No, I don't. I want..." He swallowed. "Something I don't deserve."

"What don't you deserve?" she whispered.

Wrapping his arms around her, Jason drew her closer, resting his chin gently in her hair. "A second chance."

TWENTY-SIX

"**R**eady?"

Jace was standing on the threshold of Emily's front door, shifting his weight, and wiping sweaty palms on his pants like he was picking up a date for prom. He managed a smile as she grabbed her purse and cell.

"I'll see you later, sweet boy," she said, bending to pet Snaggles.

"There's a new Indian restaurant on Seventeenth," Jace said as they got into his Jeep. "I haven't been there, but the reviews say it's good."

"Sounds great."

Jace seemed lost in his own thoughts, hands on the wheel, gaze on the road ahead. The streetlights slid by, illuminating the shallow puddles left by the late afternoon storm.

As much as she tried to process the fact that she agreed to go out to dinner with her ex-fiancé, every time she turned to glance at Jace's silhouette framed by the Jeep's dashboard lights, shock rippled through her. Shock, terror, and an undeniable sense of *this is right.*

"Jace?"

His eyebrow lifted in question.

"I don't know how to do this," Emily said into the space between them.

Jace took a deep breath, eyes still on the road. "That's the thing," he said. "I don't either."

She nodded. "Be patient with me."

"Of course."

Jace held the door open as they entered the restaurant, leaving behind the warm humidity for the sharply cold air conditioning inside. It was a cozy little place, with tables draped in cream tablecloths and elephants carved into the backs of the padded wooden chairs. With a soft smile, he pulled one out and motioned for her to sit.

The server delivered the menu before silently slipping away to bring ice waters.

"Jace, more than half the menu is vegan," Emily said wonderingly. "I love it."

He nodded. "I didn't know if you still ate a plant-based diet, but I figured that even if you didn't, you'd be able to find something you'd enjoy," he said.

A tad better than being force-fed a hamburger after being plied by alcohol.

They fell into easy conversation, and before Emily realized it, they were on their way back to her townhouse and Jace was walking her to her front door.

"Next week, same time, same place?" he asked as she unlocked the door.

"That sounds perfect."

He took a step forward then stopped, his gaze dipping to her mouth.

Does he want to kiss me? I want him to want to kiss me, right? Right?

Emily took a hesitant step toward him.

"We're not friends," she said.

"No," Jason said. "We're not."

He took a tentative step closer.

His cell phone buzzed. As he pulled it out of his pocket and said *hello*, she slipped through the door and locked it firmly behind her.

The *blub-blub-blub* of a diesel engine throbbed lazily through the window open to the early-evening air. Frowning at the sound, Emily pushed the curtain aside to peer out her mom's living room.

"What is that?" Emily asked.

Her mom snuck in beside her. "That, my dear daughter, looks like a Ford truck and a horse trailer."

"Why is it backing up in Jace's driveway?"

Before her mom had a chance to answer, Emily dashed out the screen door and onto the back deck. Whoever was driving the enormous black truck was straightening out the trailer and angling it expertly, lining the back doors up with the edge of the driveway as if they intended to unload its contents right onto the sand.

To Emily's surprise, Tyler emerged from the truck in a plaid button-down shirt, nearly-too-tight Wrangler jeans, and—God help her—*a cowboy hat.* Her mouth fell open.

Where the hell is Jess? Because if I'm enjoying the view, I can only imagine what she would say.

Tyler slammed the driver's side door shut and glanced over to Emily, smiling as he made his way to the back of the trailer.

"Hey," he said as if horse trailers, giant black trucks, and gorgeous men in cowboy hats appearing in the next-door neighbor's driveway happened every day.

Emily snapped her mouth shut. "Uh, hi, Tyler."

With a cocky smile, Tyler tipped his hat, unlocked the trailer doors, and led a horse out. It waited patiently along the side of the driveway as he went back inside and guided a second one onto the sand.

Molly bounded onto Jace's deck and stopped at the railing to watch Tyler and the two horses. Jace appeared a moment later.

"Hey, Em," he called.

She waved back tentatively.

Her mom emerged from the cottage and came up beside her, wine glass in hand. "You look like a fish," she whispered before taking a sip, her eyes on the horses.

Emily snapped her mouth shut again.

"Hi, Jason," her mom called with a wave.

"Hello, Mrs. Lanson," he called back. "What do you think, Em? Would you enjoy a ride down the beach this evening?"

Her mom leaned close. "If you don't say yes, I will," her mom whispered.

"And to think," Emily whispered back. "He's not even a fireman."

Emily straightened her shirt and glanced around for her sneakers. "Sure," she called. "I'll be right over."

A moment later she was standing next to Tyler and the two horses, a dun and a bay.

"I have a couple of soft saddles or bareback pads—your choice," Tyler said as he held the reins of both animals. Realizing that Emily didn't know what either was, he continued, "A soft saddle has stirrups. The pads don't. Might be easier to mount with the saddle if it's been a while since you rode."

"Soft saddle for me, then," Emily said.

Jace retrieved two generously padded black saddles from the back seat of Tyler's truck.

"Which one should I ride?" Emily asked as she scratched the nose of the bay.

"They have similar temperaments," Tyler said. "The bay is Duke, and the dun is Ember. They're both pretty mellow. They're used to the tide and less experienced riders, so you shouldn't have any problems with either of them."

"Then I'll take Duke, here," Emily said.

After Tyler secured the soft saddle, she mounted Duke—and sighed. There was nothing like being on a horse on a beach with the sun sinking toward the horizon and the waves gently tumbling around you.

Well, nothing like being on a horse at sunset with the man that I've always… No. Stop that, Emily. Stop it right now.

"See you in a few," Jace said to his cousin as he swung up onto the dun.

"I'll be here," Tyler said, settling into Jace's porch swing and taking off his hat.

The sun dipped toward the water as they traveled south. On their left, the thin forest of the state park leaned toward the receding tide. As Tyler had promised, the mounts were calm and forgiving, and she and Jace rode unhurriedly and steadily along the sand.

Jace brought his horse alongside hers.

"Thank you," she said. "I don't remember the last time I rode. Charles doesn't like any kind of animals, even horses and—you know what? Never mind. None of that matters. Just—thanks."

He nodded and then said, "I should have done this sooner."

She looked out to the Gulf. "We were supposed to ride in

Mexico, the day after, you know..."

Jace paled. "I didn't mean—"

Shaking her head, Emily said, "No, no, it's fine. I can talk about it now. It's...better."

He nodded, following her gaze to the horizon.

"Can we stop and watch the sun go down?" she asked.

As they paused as the bottom of the sun lightly kissed the water, she reached out for Jace's hand and found it was already waiting for hers.

It had been three days since their horseback ride alongside the state park, and Emily could think of hardly anything but the feel of Jace's hand in hers.

Warm. Strong. Familiar.

Right.

Her doorbell rang.

Emily took a deep breath and opened the door. Jace was leaning against the townhouse's stucco wall, a tentative smile curving his full lips. His eyes sparkled. A light blue button-down shirt—rolled almost to the elbow—strained against his biceps in the most perfect of ways. Her belly did a little swoop.

Jace, as promised, was early.

"Hey," she said.

"Hey, yourself," he said, offering her a bouquet tied with a cream ribbon. "These are for you."

"Peonies?" she asked, her eyes widening a fraction. "You remembered."

Snaggles waddled up to the open door. "Hey, buddy," Jace said, bending down to greet the little dog as she searched for a vase for the flowers.

"Would you like to go back to the Indian restaurant or try

something new?" he asked.

"Is it okay if we go back there?"

Smiling knowingly, he said, "Sure."

The restaurant was only ten minutes from her townhouse. Jace seemed strangely nervous on the drive, silent and avoiding her gaze.

Why was he nervous? *It's me*, she wanted to say. *It's us.*

His right elbow rested on the center panel; his hand was free. She wanted to take it in hers and thread her fingers with his.

Do it, you idiot. He's letting you lead. He's waiting for you to reach for him, just like on the beach. He's been waiting for you to kiss him, too.

Remembering Jace answering his cell phone when he dropped her off at home after their last dinner date, she folded her arms, tucked her fingers away, and turned away to gaze out the passenger side window.

More silence punctuated by the click of the Jeep's turn signal.

The whir of the car's air conditioner.

The thrum of the tires along the road.

Within another couple minutes, Jace had pulled into the restaurant's parking lot, and they were walking inside.

"Our apologies," the host said. "We had some water damage during yesterday's storm, so our dining room is closed. The kitchen is open for takeout, however."

Emily glanced at Jace. "What do you think?"

"We can eat on my deck, if that's okay. There shouldn't be too many mosquitoes tonight."

Back at his cottage, Emily spooned the tikka masala, vegetable korma, and basmati rice into bowls, then arranged the samosas on a plate as Jace opened a bottle of red wine.

"How's the unpacking going?" he asked as he poured two

glasses.

"Okay. It's taking longer than I hoped because some of the boxes didn't get put in the right rooms."

"I'm happy to come over and move things around for you, if that helps. Whatever you need."

Emily blinked. "Sure."

"How about Sunday after brunch?"

"Thanks," she said, bringing the food out to the deck.

The breeze accompanied their light conversation until it was too dark to see, and they brought their empty plates inside.

Jace slipped back out the slider and onto the deck, giving her a chance to roam the kitchen alone.

A square, deep brown table, with two chairs.

Two sets of dishes in the sink. Two wine glasses.

A mother dog and her pups, curled up next to each other, asleep.

What could have been. What *should* have been.

An ache spread from beneath her ribs, filling her chest with a searing pang of loss. Is this what their home would be like if they had married eight years ago? Even if...even if somehow, miraculously, they were able to work things out now, how would she be able to let go of the feeling that she'd—*they'd*—been robbed of eight years of—

The slider opened and Jace entered the kitchen.

He glanced at her. "Em?"

She offered him what she hoped was an encouraging smile. "I'm okay."

Stopping across the room from her, he nodded, grimacing. "Will you—are you up for—would you like to stay for a movie?"

Emily walked over to him and reached for his hand. "Sure. You pick, though."

Hand in hand, Jace led her to the living room, and she tucked herself into the couch. He sat down a foot from her, leaving his arm extended along the back of the cushions.

"Closer," he murmured.

At his words, Emily's stomach somersaulted. She scooted toward Jace, and he slid his arm around her.

Swallowing against a dry throat, she asked, "Can you just hold me? That's…that's all I want to do right now."

Emily felt him stiffen and gently move his arm. "Is this okay?" he asked.

"Yeah," she whispered. "In fact…" She laid down, her head on his lap, keeping her eyes on the movie.

His fingers found their way into her curls, threading through them gently. Methodically.

Bliss.

After a few minutes, she sat up.

He put his arm around her; she snuggled closer. He turned, his gaze fixed on her mouth.

"Jace," she whispered. "Don't. Not yet."

She saw the question on his lips—*when?*

"I know it's hard to trust me," he said, his words breaking her heart.

"It is."

"Take all the time you need," he said. "When you're ready, I'm here."

"Don't give up on me, Jace. I just need time." She reached up to trace the edge of his jaw with her fingertip. "It won't be long, I promise."

TWENTY-SEVEN

It had been more than eight years since Emily had awoken in the safety of Jace's arms.

It felt like yesterday. And a lifetime ago.

Blinking at the sun streaming in the bay window, she nestled nearer, doing her best not to wake him. His hair was tousled in the most endearing of ways, the lines on his face—new these last years—softened by sleep.

She never dreamed she'd wake here. Yawning, she turned over and snuggled closer into his chest. The puppies at her feet wiggled, repositioned themselves, and immediately fell back asleep.

Emily traced the line of his bicep with her finger, moving up until it touched the patterned ink encircling his arm. He watched her intently, eyes glittering.

"When did you get your tattoo?" she asked sleepily.

"Tyler, Jessie, and I got them the same day a few years back. His matches Jessie's."

She lifted her head off Jace's chest and turned to look him in the eye. "I'm sorry? What?"

"Tyler and Jessie have matching tattoos. Hers

isn't…usually visible," he said, his face reddening. "I thought she would have told you."

"Nope."

Emily laid back on his chest, thoughts reeling, as she felt her face drain of color.

Wait. Does someone have a matching—

She had to know. No matter if it hurt more than she could imagine. She steeled herself for the answer to the question she had to ask.

"So, Tyler and Jess have matching tattoos. Who has the tattoo that matches yours?"

Jace pulled his arm tighter around her, the deep murmur of his voice making his chest rumble. "No one yet."

Oh.

Rising from the couch, Jason took a step and landed on a dog toy. Wincing, he said, "I have to find homes for the final two puppies. As soon as I can."

"Why don't you have a housewarming party?" Emily asked.

Jace raised an eyebrow. "What were you thinking?"

"I don't know. It might be fun to have some people over for a barbeque or something. You could show everyone the puppies. You're bound to get takers. Even if they're both not adopted, they're so cute I'm sure the word will get out."

"Not a bad idea," he conceded. "When?"

"How about Sunday? We could have brunch here instead of at Gulf and Main. We could get Cass to cater it, so we don't have to cook."

We? I wonder if he caught that.

"That would work with the age of the puppies. One more week after that and they'll be ready for their new homes."

"Who should we—uh, you—invite?" Emily asked.

Dammit! Conversations with this man are a minefield.

"I'd like to keep it small, so Tyler, Callie, Mel, and Kathleen," he said. "And Cass, of course."

"Tell them all to bring a guest," Emily said. "And I'll tell Jessie."

"I'll ask Cass about catering the food. Would you like me to order all vegan? I'm happy to."

Emily's heart warmed at his words. "You don't need to. A dish or two would be fine. I don't want a revolt on my hands."

Jace chuckled. "Never."

"What are you doing this afternoon? Do you mind coming over to the townhouse and helping me move some furniture and boxes around?"

"Sure." He walked into the kitchen, and she heard a curse. "Em," he called. "I have some bad news." Reappearing in the doorway to the living room, he continued, "I'm out of coffee."

"We could walk to a coffee shop," she said. "I still have some stuff over at Mom's. Let me grab a change of clothes and meet you back here in a few."

"I think most of those are books," Em said, pointing at the stacks of boxes in the dining room then pulling her curls into a ponytail. She smiled. "I...um, have a lot of them."

Jason was standing in the middle of Em's townhouse in a sea of cardboard and packing paper, looking around for the next thing to help her with. He'd already rearranged the living room furniture and assembled her kitchen table. Unpacking books seemed like a decent project to tackle next.

"Well, that's easy. I'll start opening the boxes," he said. "We can get the books on the shelves tonight and get all the boxes broken down and out of here. You'll have a lot more space then."

He reached for the box on top.

"Not that one."

Her words were suddenly cold. Bitter.

"Where does this one belong?" he asked, bewildered at her sudden change in tone.

"You can put it in my bedroom. But that one stays permanently sealed."

Jason nodded and carried it to Em's bedroom. The box had been opened and resealed more than once. As he put it down, he noticed what was written on the side in thick, black marker:

Cancún. Do not open.

Shit. Shit. Shit.
What was in there?

TWENTY-EIGHT

The day of the barbeque, Jason was standing on his deck squinting in the late afternoon sun when Cass walked up the driveway.

"Hey," she called. "Where do you want the food?"

"You can put it in the kitchen. I'll open the garage door so you can come through there," he called back.

Jason held the door from the garage to the kitchen open, and Cass shouldered her way in, a covered aluminum tray in her hands. Ryan followed with another. The police officer placed his gently on the counter and shook hands with Jason.

"I should have left the big guy at Gulf and Main," Cass groused, nodding in Ryan's direction. "Since my place is open and I'm not there."

"I'm sure the pub is in capable hands," Jason said.

Ryan added, "It's good to take a day off every now and again."

Cass grunted.

"The food smells delicious," Jason offered.

"I happen to know what you guys like from the menu. There are two—no, make that three more trays," she said.

"I'll get them," Ryan said, disappearing into the garage.

"So, you two—" Jason began, giving his friend a crooked smile.

"You stop right there," she said.

"See, you sound like a cop alread—"

"Not funny, Jason."

"But—"

Ryan returned bearing another tray. "You know Cassidy here isn't fond of people teasing her," he said, eyes twinkling, as he turned back to the garage.

For a moment, he was alone with Em in the kitchen.

He watched her as she opened bottles of wine and stacked napkins, as naturally as if it were her cottage. *Their* cottage.

Puppies barked. Ice clinked against glasses. Laughter leaked in from the deck.

It was obvious.

Em needed to be there permanently.

She needed to be *his* permanently.

Somehow.

Don't get ahead of yourself, he thought. *You haven't even kissed her yet. At least not in the last eight years.*

After encouraging everyone to start eating, Jason wandered into the living room. Kathleen was in the corner on the floor, playing with Milo. Callie and Mel were conspiring on the couch, glancing at him furtively and whispering.

He retreated to the deck.

Tyler was chatting with Em, his arm draped around her best friend. His cousin was looking rather pleased with himself.

"So, when's your next trip to Africa?" Em asked as Jason joined them.

"Not for a couple months. I haven't finished processing

the raw images from my last trip yet," Tyler said.

"I saw your book over at Jess's. The photos are gorgeous," Em continued.

"Thank you," he said, his eyes never leaving Jessie as if the last word Em had spoken reminded him to gaze at the woman at his side.

"So glad you guys could make it," Jason said, stepping closer to Em.

Tyler shrugged. "I was in town," he said.

A tug on his arm accompanied by a stunning smile pulled him away from the conversation. Callie.

"Could I borrow you for a sec?" she asked.

Jace followed her to the kitchen. She leaned toward him as if she was going to divulge her deepest secrets, her blonde curls captured in a messy ponytail. "Mel told me that you have one appointment tomorrow at 10:45 and another one at noon," she said quietly. "Both routine exams. I'm rescheduling them. Well, technically, Mel is rescheduling them."

"Callie, what—"

"There are no patients in the kennel, so you don't have to come in Monday night, either," she whispered.

"But—"

"*Jason Williams.* Don't make me use your full name. I despise doing that." She pursed her lips then a moment later, gave him a wicked, knowing smile. "Any fool can see what's happening here. Take the rest of today—and tomorrow, too—and figure out what you have to do to get her back."

Jason let out a long breath. "Thanks, Callie."

"You got it. Now I'm going to chase the rest of the people out of here as soon as possible so you can be alone with her."

Emily cleaned up the kitchen as well as she could, then wandered around Jace's cottage, half-full wine glass in hand, collecting abandoned plates and dirty glasses to bring to the sink. Jace had tried to help, but she'd insisted he socialize with the last two guests—Cass and Ryan—before they left for the evening.

She wanted to be alone, if just for a moment. The swell of emotion that seemed to crash into her chest every time she took a breath was almost too much to bear.

The slightest nudge would launch her relationship with Jace into everything they knew before. It was like rereading a favorite book, starting at chapter three.

She hoped this time the ending would be different.

She paused at the sliding glass door.

Jace was on the deck, alone.

The ache under her ribs roared to life, taunting her. Once more, it murmured of promise and loss; an inevitable future with Jace, irrevocably tethered to mourning for *what could have been*.

Potential happiness mingled with grief for the loss of eight years.

She tamped down the sadness and took a deep breath.

A tear slipped from her eye as she slid the door open.

Jace's eyes were on the waves, somewhere out where water met sky. He turned to look at her, something in his gaze she couldn't decipher.

As she looked at him, she felt the last of her resistance crumble.

Jace—

"Stay," he whispered.

It was both a plea and a command.

Her belly dropped to her knees.

She took a hesitant step toward the man who had ruined her heart.

He reached for her. His fingertips tucked a wayward curl behind her ear and traced the curve of her jaw.

A tear tumbled down her cheek and landed on Jace's arm. "Em?"

"If you leave again, I won't survive it," she whispered. "I'm not sure I did last time."

He leaned closer until his forehead gently touched hers. "I can't ever make it up to you," he whispered. "But I'm sure as hell going to try."

There was something in Em's eyes beneath the tears that hadn't been there before.

Forgiveness, maybe? A spark of desire?

Jason reached up to cup her cheek and her eyes slid shut. She angled her head and leaned into his hand. He drew closer, close enough to feel her breath against his lips, and gave her the span of a heartbeat to pull away. When she didn't, he closed the space between them as if it had never been there. Then—ever so gently—touched his lips to hers.

He waited.

She was stock-still.

Another breath.

Then—

Jace felt her lips move beneath his. Tentatively, at first.

A moment later, they parted for him, inviting him in as her fingers slowly tangled in his hair, dragging him closer.

Suddenly, there was nothing but the unmistakable taste of her lips, the feel of her familiar embrace. It threatened to reduce him to tears.

Em—*his* Em.

He groaned, bringing both hands alongside her face, combing his fingers through her curls, deepening the kiss, hungrily giving and taking until they were both gasping, breathless.

Panting, she broke the kiss and stepped away.

He took her in, hair tousled, lips swollen, breath fast, eyes dark with desire.

His Em—perfection itself.

Taking her hand, Jason led her inside.

As Emily laced her fingers in Jace's and followed him down the tiny hall toward his bedroom, she realized there was something in his touch that had never been there before; something in his shaking fingertips that bordered on *reverence*. A gentleness born, perhaps, of the hurt that he had caused.

Jace paused at the bedroom's threshold as if he knew another step would commit them to the future they had once wanted more than anything else in the world.

Slipping past him, Emily led him toward the bed.

The room felt bare and sparse around her; the only nod to comfort were thick curtains softening the sides of the window and the rug at her feet.

Turning, she stepped into his embrace. He met her lips with his own. At first, his kiss was as soft as a familiar whisper. Then, with the tremble of a tiny earthquake, Jace angled his head to deepen their kiss.

She was consumed by it.

For minutes.

Hours.

A lifetime.

Breathless, she pulled away.

He traced the line of her jaw with his fingertip, down her

neck to the curve of her shoulder. Emily lowered herself onto the comforter, and Jace released her hand and stepped away. An ache for his touch welled like a tide as she watched him pad to the nightstand, lit by a solitary lamp, and turn it off with a soft *snick*.

She traced his steps in the darkness as he found his way back to her, and she stood to meet him.

He stopped.

And waited.

As Emily looked up at him in the darkness, she unbuttoned her shirt, and it fell away under his touch, drifting past her shoulders and floating to the floor.

Jace hooked his finger under the waist of her shorts and tugged gently.

A request.

A plea.

A memory skidded across her thoughts, of a night like this one, air stirring in a lazy breeze, filled with gentle sighs and even gentler touches. Touches that started tenderly, ultimately giving way to the raw need borne of their desire for one another.

She unzipped her shorts, dragged them down her legs, and stepped out of them, reaching for Jace's shirt.

Buttons were her newest enemy.

He watched her fingers work from beneath long eyelashes, his chest quivering under heavy breaths, as if he were about to explode.

When she was finished, he shrugged off his button-down shirt and stepped away, crossing his arms, and yanking off his white undershirt to toss it aside.

Emily drank in the sight of him: his achingly familiar body honed into perfection, all planes and angles, solid and unyielding. Reaching out, she traced the deep lines in the shape of a V, dipping below his abs and disappearing under his shorts. His eyes slid shut as he shuddered under her attention, as if he were fighting to keep a thin veneer of control—stretched over all-consuming hunger—firmly in place.

She stepped away and he bent to put his lips on hers, touching her only with his kiss.

Standing in the darkness in Jace's bedroom.

His mouth exploring hers.

Jace—

The ghost of a touch skittered across her skin as he traced her shoulder blades with a fingertip.

She shivered.

In one swift motion, Jace stepped out of his shorts and leaned forward to take her mouth again. An eternity of kisses, each deeper than the last.

Each leaving her wanting more. And more.

With a groan, Jace broke their kiss and stepped away, breathing hard. He hooked his finger on her panties and tugged.

Another question.

"Please," she breathed. "Please."

Ever so slowly, Jace dragged her panties down her thighs.

She would die of want.

Gradually, she backed away from him until her legs collided with his mattress. As she sank into the comforter, the smell of him blinded her to everything but his touch.

In the near darkness, Jace bent down onto his knees. He gently prodded her legs until they parted for him, his tongue trailing a path up the inside of her calf to her thigh.

She bit her lip to keep from crying out.

When he put his lips on her—exploring, delving, discovering her again—the entire world was reduced to his touch.

There—

An involuntary gasp escaped her.

Whimpering, she tangled her fingers in his hair as a deluge of passion claimed every thought.

"Jace…" she managed with a strangled cry, dragging herself up as he pulled away, eyes half-lidded with his own need to continue.

She tugged on the waistband of his underwear. Jace pulled them off and moved toward her.

"Wait," she breathed. "I want to look at you."

Straightening, he offered her a cocky, crooked smile.

He was hard angles, sharp jawlines, and smooth, sleek muscle. Beyond magnificent.

Enough looking.

Emily slid back on the bed and murmured, "Come here."

In a breath, he obliged, the velvet and satin of his skin covering hers as he draped himself above her. Silk stretched over iron.

A thrill of anticipation.

A rush of fresh desire.

Intoxicated, she melted into him, not knowing—not caring—where she ended and he began.

Jace was so gentle, it was breaking her heart.

And driving her stark raving insane.

Needing more of him, Emily froze, cupping his face in both her hands and forcing him to pause and look her in the eye. "Don't hold back," she whispered raggedly.

Something in his gaze changed. She arched her back and let him—

White-hot need rippled through her, and then she was falling off an endless cliff, dragging Jace with her.

Panting, he touched his forehead against hers and smiled

softly.

With a murmured sigh, Jace curled up behind her, wrapped his arms around her, and dragged her close, nothing between them any longer.

"I love you," she whispered.

Jace pulled her closer to his chest. "Do you think you're ready?" he whispered.

"For what?"

"For everything."

TWENTY-NINE

It was hours before Emily and Jace managed to extract themselves—rather reluctantly, but sated, giddy, and hopeful—from his bed.

"Brunch at Gulf and Main?" he asked, glancing at the bedside alarm clock.

"Sure," Emily said. "Walk or drive?"

"Drive." She offered Jace a coy smile. "I'm a little tired this morning. Someone kept me up far past my bedtime."

He chuckled.

"Not that I'm complaining," she added.

"Not that you're complaining," he echoed, suppressing a smile. "Because you certainly weren't complaining last night."

When they made it to Gulf and Main's parking lot, he parked the Jeep, and jogged around to open her door, offering his hand to help her out of the car. Smiling, she threaded her fingers with his.

A white Subaru slowed down as it passed by on Main Street.

Mike Malone.

"Was that—"

"I think so," Emily said.

"I have no words," he growled. "I can't believe that asshole is walking around free. He should be in jail."

Emily squeezed Jace's hand. "We don't have to think about him ever again."

Fingers laced together, they walked into the pub.

"Two house margaritas, Cass," Jace said as they slid into their favorite barstools.

"Nope," Cass said, hands on the bar, shaking her head, mischief in her eyes.

"Are you out of tequila? Or am I out of credit?"

"You'll never be out of credit here," Cass replied with a sly smile. "And I will never be out of tequila." She dropped a single, large ice cube in each of two highball glasses, set them on the bar, and disappeared into the backroom without a word.

Emily glanced at Jace, eyebrows raised.

A moment later, Cass returned with a skinny black box with an elongated oval label and set it on the bar in front of them. "I've been meaning to get to a liquor store and get you two something special…"

"You remembered," Jace said, a smile warming his face as he opened the box and withdrew a deep brown bottle of Lagavulin. "Thanks, Cass."

"I figured you guys were sick of the margaritas but were too nice to say anything about it," she said.

"Nonsense," Jason said. "Your margaritas are exceptional."

He opened the bottle and poured a glass for Emily, who sighed appreciatively as she brought the Scotch to her lips.

"One for you?" he asked Cass.

"Sure," she said and placed a cube in another glass.

After taking a sip, Cass said, "Great stuff."

"Takes years for it to be this good," Emily added.

Jason raised his glass and met Em's eye. "The best things are worth the wait."

Cass offered them a rare smile, and then disappeared into the back.

Jace leaned over and kissed her softly, and from across the bar came a gasp, followed by a delighted squeak.

Callie came bouncing over in a blinding lime minidress, the color of a yellow-green firetruck. "It's official!" she squealed.

"What's—"

She bounded away before Jace could finish his question.

Callie returned with a reluctant Cass in tow. "Can you see it? It's the most beautiful, most spectacular hue I've ever seen!"

"What—" Emily tried.

"What—" Jason started.

"Your auras! They're purple!" Callie cried.

Jace, Cass, and Emily looked at each other in confusion.

"For Pete's sake, people!" Callie said, rolling her eyes. "Purple means you're in love!"

Several hours later—after returning from Gulf and Main and getting rather distracted by the bed—and then the sofa— Jason watched Em back out of his driveway and turn left onto Gulf Road.

They'd spent the rest of the day mostly in bed, rising only to wander into the kitchen in search of food.

He didn't want her to go.

He never wanted to watch her leave again.

As her taillights disappeared around the corner, his thoughts returned to the only one thing he could do to keep her here—permanently.

But if he was going to pull it off, he was going to need help.

THIRTY

"So, what did you want to talk to me about?"

Jason dropped down at Em's best friend's kitchen table and leaned back in his chair.

It had been difficult to pin down Jessie at home and sneak in a visit without Em finding out. The woman seemed to have no regular schedule. How Em could endure her best friend's antics—when she needed perfect order to her world—was beyond him.

But now that he was here, Jason wasn't sure how to begin.

"I want to plan a surprise for Em," he said levelly.

As if that were the half of it.

"What kind of surprise?"

Jason leaned forward, resting his elbows on the table. Something crunched underneath them. The remains of breakfast? Last week's dinner? He winced and tried to ignore whatever was now sticking to the bottom of his elbows.

"What was Emily's wedding like?"

"Excuse me?" Jessie said.

"Her wedding to Charles Driscoll. What was it like?"

Jessie blinked. "Well…" She paused, as if trying to figure out what to share. "It was big. Like hundreds and hundreds of people big. All the standard stuff you would expect, but way over the top. Giant poufy Cinderella dress. Stretch limos. Two live bands. The works." Jessie tipped her head to the side. "Why?"

Curious. That didn't sound like what he and Em had planned for their wedding eight years ago in Cancún. The woman he knew had never been a fan of big weddings. Had things changed? Would a small wedding to Charles have reminded her of what he'd done? Had she wanted the opposite of everything that had shattered her heart?

Shit, what was he thinking? There was no way he could pull this off without hurting Em in some way.

Jessie took a bite of an apple then continued. "The thing is, Em didn't want any of that. She wanted *simple*. A handful of close friends and family. No fanfare. Just the important stuff, she always said. But Charles wanted epic proportions. That's who he is. Think of the most audacious, extravagant, ridiculous thing you can, and you'll be on the right track." Jessie shrugged. "Eventually, Em caved. She didn't feel like a single day was worth fighting about for months."

"Again," Jessie said, leaning forward this time. "Why do you ask?"

Jason swallowed. *It's now or never, big guy. Here we go.*

"I'm going to plan the wedding Em always wanted—the wedding she didn't get, but deserved," he said. "And it's going to be a surprise."

If one thing could be said about Em's best friend, it would be that she could take things in stride.

Jessie stared at Jason until he began to squirm.

"I have to say that I don't know what to say," she finally said.

"Fair enough," Jason replied.

"Okay. Scratch that. I figured out what to say. First question: are you out of your damn mind?"

Jason sighed. "I might be."

Jessie rose from the table and planted her hands on her hips. "Second question: are you out of your damn mind?"

"Look," he continued. "I want to marry her. And I know she wants to spend the rest of her life with me. The problem is, if we plan a wedding, the whole Cancún thing is going to surface again. I want to marry her without putting her through all that."

Em's best friend grunted a reply. Then: "Admirable. And stupid as the day is long."

"Right." He dragged his hands through his hair. "Jessie, help me. I need the low-down. How is Em going to react?"

"Honestly? I don't know," she hedged, staring at him. "You're one hundred percent sure about this?"

"Yeah."

"I mean, if you're wrong, and she doesn't want to marry you, what happens then? You will have embarrassed her with all her friends there to witness it..." Jessie shook her head. "You'll be up shits creek without an anchor, and you'll have hurt her again—badly. And in a similar way."

"True."

"And if you hurt her, I swear to you, I will find that whatever-the-hell-you-call-it that Ty has in his barn for gelding horses and I swear, even though I assume you're not horse-sized, I'll figure out how to use it on you."

"I know." He met Jessie's eye. "I saw a box at Em's place with 'Cancún' written on it. She didn't want to unpack it. Do you know what's inside?"

"Of course, I do. I helped her pack it," Jessie said.

"Well…?"

"Oh, so you want me to tell you what's in it?" She gave him a strange look. "You sure you want to know?"

Jason pursed his lips and bit back a feeling of foreboding. "I do."

Her eyebrow lifted. "Em calls it her Graveyard of Wedding Dreams, or something like that. It's all her things that remind her of you—or her ex-husband. Her sandals from Cancún. The photos of her wedding to Charles. Stuff like that. Things she couldn't bring herself to throw out."

"Damn," Jason muttered.

"I told her that someday she might be okay with seeing all of it again, and that she might regret getting rid of it in the middle of, well, all the heartbreak."

"She loved that engagement ring you gave her, you know," Jessie continued, sighing. "She said that every time she looked at it, she remembered the look on your face when you went down on your knee and asked her to marry you," she said. "After Cancún, we collected the bad juju stuff in a cardboard box and sealed it up, and after her divorce from Charles, she pulled it out from the back of her closet and put in some more random things from that disaster on top. Inside the box is kinda like a layer cake of pain."

"Well, shit."

"Exactly." Jessie appraised him over the rim of her Coke can. "It's emotional baggage, except it's, well, physical."

"Right," Jason said, letting out a long breath and dragging his hands through his hair again. After a moment, he said, "I need you to get the box for me."

"Excuse me?"

"Just for a day," he insisted.

"What? No. Not going to happen."

"I'll return it when I'm done, minus one small thing."

"Dude, just so we're clear, the stuff in that box does not belong to you."

"I know. I just thought—"

"I'm pretty sure whatever is going on in your pretty little head right now does not classify as 'thinking'."

"You said she loved the ring I gave her, right?"

Jessie tilted her head and appraised him as if she were trying to decide whether he was insane or not. "I don't think I need to tell you how devastated she was when the whole Cancún thing went down," she said. "But the stuff in that box is hers. Opening that box without her permission isn't right, never mind taking—"

"Borrowing," he corrected.

"—taking something out of it. You can't just help yourself to someone else's personal stuff, no matter how small. And on the outside chance that you don't know, it's called 'stealing'."

"Tell me something, Jessie," Jason said. "If I'm able to pull off this surprise wedding and Em and I get married, do you think she'd want to wear that ring?"

Jessie groaned. "Just so you know, I hate you." She got up from the table and looked out the window. "Em's townhouse is neater than my grandma's sock drawer. She'll notice if the box is missing. And I'll get caught."

"What if—"

"No. Absolutely not."

"I want you to picture Em's face when she sees that engagement ring on her finger again."

"I thought you were a vet. Are you in sales now or something?"

"I only want to take the ring to a jeweler. They can measure its size and then I can find a wedding band to match.

Then you—"

"I'm not involved in your heist, Danny Ocean."

"Then you can put the ring back. After the wedding, I'll ask her if she still has the engagement ring, and if she wants to wear it, she can get it out of the box."

Jessie huffed annoyingly. "Tell you what, you major annoyance of a human," she said. "This is extremely inconvenient. *You* are extremely inconvenient."

"But will you help me?"

Jessie let out a long, drawn-out groan, and let her head drop into her hands. "Do I have a choice?"

Staring at the kitchen ceiling, she finished her apple as Jason sat silently, waiting.

"What will she wear?" Jessie mumbled.

Jason raised an eyebrow.

She met his eye. "The bride needs a dress, for heaven's sake, you idiotic, oblivious male."

"I hadn't figured that one out. It's not like I can ask Em for her size without ruining the surprise."

"All right. I know how to take care of that one," she said. "I only have one more question for you," Jessie said. "When?"

"Will you be in town on the eighteenth?"

Jason was parked next to his cousin at the bar at Gulf and Main, not at all looking forward to what Tyler was about to say.

"Yup. Why?"

"I'm planning a wedding," Jason said.

"For whom?"

"For Em and me. I'm going to surprise her."

Tyler blinked. "Are you out of your fucking mind?"

"Maybe. Probably. Likely."

Tyler took a long swallow of beer. "Look, before you do this, you need to figure out what happened last time. Why you ran."

"I know what happened," Jason said.

"Care to fill me in?"

"Cold feet."

"You *disappeared*. Not only on Emily, but everyone. That's not garden-variety cold feet, cuz. That's psycho-level bullshit and it ruined your fiancé's life for years." Tyler stared at him. "Whatever it was that made you leave, you need to get it out of your head, so there's no chance you'll do it again."

Jason pursed his lips. "I'm good, cuz. I'm telling you."

Tyler nodded slowly. "Did you tell Jess?"

"Yeah."

"What did she say?"

"She asked me if I was out of my damn mind. And you asked me if I was out of my fucking mind. You guys really should coordinate your responses better."

Tyler snorted. "Is Connor coming?"

Jason huffed at the mention of his brother. "Not sure, but he's on assignment, so likely not."

Silence.

"So, will you be there?" Jason asked after a moment.

Nodding, Tyler said, "Sure. If nothing more than to hold things together when everything goes to shit."

THIRTY-ONE

The heavy, metal-edged glass door thumped into its frame behind Jason as he strode into the florist on the corner of Sixteenth and Main, the ice-cold air conditioning fogging up his sunglasses. He took them off and glanced around. Peonies, identical to the ones he'd given Em on their first date, glanced up at him from the refrigerator case. Maybe he'd grab a few more before he left.

"Hello," a woman's voice called from the back. "I'll be with you in one moment."

Danny's Lions was a cute little place two doors down from Gulf and Main, nestled between a coffee shop and a boutique clothing store, its shelves stocked with picture frames and knickknacks, statues and vases, mugs and mirrors, and, of course, hundreds of flowers.

A woman appeared, her bright green apron damp and peppered with fragments of leaves from whatever plant she'd been cutting in the back room.

"How may I help you?"

A southern accent and warm smile softened her question.

"I would like to order a bouquet and a vase of flowers for

a week from Saturday."

"Absolutely." She nodded toward a table and chairs. "Would you like to sit while we discuss the specifics of your order?"

Jason nodded.

"You're interested in a bouquet and an arrangement," the woman said, taking notes in long, smooth strokes. "What's the occasion?"

"A surprise wedding."

Her pen paused mid-stroke. "And you're the…"

"Groom," he said.

The florist put her pen down and wiped her hand on her apron. "I'm Hope," she said.

He held out his hand for her to shake. "Jason Williams."

"I've never created arrangements for a surprise wedding before," she said.

"I've never gotten married in a surprise wedding before."

Hope giggled.

"I realize that florists usually need months to plan for wedding flowers," Jason said. "And I don't want you to turn me away, so I'm going small here. This is going to be a tiny wedding, anyway. Maybe a dozen guests, tops."

She offered him a smile. "But is a bouquet and a single arrangement all you truly *want*? Let's say you *did* have months. What would you order? What would make the day even more special for your bride?"

Jason shook his head. "I don't know."

"Okay," she said. "Let's start with your budget…"

"Whatever it takes," Jason said.

The florist's eyebrow lifted, and she nodded knowingly. "Let's talk about the bride's bouquet. Does she have a favorite flower?"

"She likes ranunculus and peonies," he said. "And if you

can include lilies of the valley, stephanotis, and sweet peas in the vases—depending on what you have in stock—that would be great."

The florist appraised him with a soft smile. "I'm impressed. Not many people know their partner's favorite flowers, and even fewer know the names of them."

"It's my job to know," he said simply.

Jason found himself telling their story, how they'd met and fallen in love, how they planned to marry in Mexico—and how he'd disappeared, and met again here, in the town where they'd first met years ago.

Hope listened, eyes widening as he finished.

When he was done, a boy about seven years old with eyes the color of the summer sky and sandy blond hair darted out from behind the counter, stopping behind Hope. In his hands, he held an extra-large binder filled with example wedding invitations.

"You'll want this," the boy whispered, running his fingers along the cover.

"This is my son, Danny," she said, taking the binder and setting it on the table in front of Jason. Another smile. "What will you do for invitations?"

"I looked online, but there's not enough time."

"Spend a few minutes picking out one you like," she said, opening the book. "I happen to have a degree in graphic design and a calligraphy hobby that tries to take over my life every once in a while. I can cook up something similar and create a dozen."

"I couldn't ask you to do that," Jason said.

"It seems I have a soft spot for surprise weddings," she said.

Jason pictured Em on the beach in a white dress, holding a bouquet, her eyes bright with the promise of a future with him. "I hope the bride does, too."

"More peonies?" Em asked with a smile so perfect, it made Jason's heart skip a beat.

Jason brushed her hair behind her shoulder. "I have something planned for you—us, I mean—a week from Saturday. A surprise."

"A surprise?"

"Yup." Smiling, Jason took a deep swallow of his coffee.

"Sounds suspicious."

"Are we headed somewhere?"

"I suppose you could say that, in a way."

"Anything in particular I need to wear? Bathing suit? Hiking shoes? Scuba gear? Sequins and stilettos?"

"Nope." He raised an eyebrow and offered her a sly smile. "But I'll never say no to you in stilettos."

His cell vibrated.

"Give me a sec," he mumbled and turned his body away, shielding the message on his cell as he typed his reply to the florist.

He saw something in her eyes as he turned back toward her.

Doubt.

"Who was that?" Em asked.

And not for the first time, he wondered if this surprise wedding would be the death of their relationship.

When Emily and Jace got to Gulf and Main, Tyler and Jess were already there, waiting for them. Jace excused himself to order their drinks at the bar and Jess went in search of the bathroom.

It was as good a time as any to ask Tyler about the steadily increasing number of texts lighting up Jace's cell.

"Can I ask you something?" she said, glancing over at Jace to make sure he was out of earshot.

"Sure," Tyler said.

"Has Jace dated anyone here?"

Jace's cousin gave her an odd look. "Do you mean has he dated anyone in Westshore Beach? I think he went out with his real estate agent. Once or twice, maybe? Other than that, not that I know of."

"Someone by the name of Hope messaged him," Emily said.

Tyler hesitated. "Doesn't he get texts from all his exes? Isn't that his thing?"

Emily felt her face flush and bit down the reply that came to mind. "He does. But something about this seemed different. He looked anxious—almost like he was trying to hide the text from me."

"Why don't you ask him directly instead of brooding about it?"

She pursed her lips. "I did. He said it was someone he met a long time ago. Except it was a local number. Something isn't adding up."

Tyler mumbled something she couldn't quite hear.

"And two weeks ago, someone named Ruby called. Another local number."

"You need to talk to Jason about it," Tyler said, looking away. "Not me."

A dozen of Hope's hand-lettered invitations sat innocently on the passenger seat next to Jason as he pulled his Jeep into the cottage's driveway. Molly and Flint greeted him at the door, following him onto the deck for some much-needed fresh air. In the distance, a storm was brewing over the Gulf. He watched the tide's path devour the beach, one of the invitations in hand.

Jason freed it from its envelope. The paper felt nearly too thick to fold, and the words were surrounded by tiny hand-painted peonies. Hope had done an incredible job.

With the sun above us and the sand below us
With our family and friends behind us and our future before us
We'll say our vows…

What the hell was he doing? Was he certain Em would agree to marry him after everything he'd put her through? Or was he going to make an ass out of himself, and everything between them worse? Or irreparable?

He turned to the sound of humming, floating in from his left. Over on her own deck, Em's mom was sitting behind an easel, dressed in a long-sleeved shirt splattered and streaked with blue and violet, a paint palette resting beside her on a wooden table.

Well, shit. It's now or never.

"Mrs. Lanson?" Emily's mom swiveled toward him and waved hello with a paintbrush wet with lilac paint. "When you have a chance, I'd love a minute of your time," he called.

She stood, analyzing the canvas she'd been working on for a moment. "I'm pretty much done," she said, looking up. "Why don't you come on over while I clean up?"

Jason grabbed an invitation, crossed the sand, and walked the steps up to what he hoped was his future mother-in-law's deck.

Jason paused to hold the door open for an elderly couple leaving Gulf and Main and glanced around before going inside. The hour between the end of Sunday brunch and the beginning of dinner was the slowest time at the pub. Only four tables were occupied, and no one was sitting at the bar. All the better. Now would be the best moment to deliver the news tucked inside in his shirt pocket.

After her initial shock wore off, Em's mom had been a fountain of support and encouragement. He could only hope the rest of their friends would react in the same way as she did.

Approaching the bar, Jason waved Cass and Callie over, and, smiling slyly, slid two thick, creamy envelopes across the wood to them.

"What's this?" Cass said, picking one up and turning it over.

"No fucking way, Jason Williams," Callie said, taking a half step back and putting her hands on her hips, "You've got to be fucking kidding me."

"You used the f-word twice and you haven't even opened it yet," Jason said. "And I have it on good authority that you don't use that word all that often."

"That's because you don't get married all that often," Callie said, launching herself over the bar and into his arms for a hug.

From behind the bar, Cass looked up from the open envelope and gasped. "Holy…"

"Will you come?" he said, his words muffled by Callie's curls. "Bear is welcome, too."

"We wouldn't miss it for the world," she said, and smiled.

The next stop was Jessie's condo.

"You did good," Jessie said after reading the invitation. "You lousy, charming, infuriating son-of-a-bitch. You actually did good."

"I only have a few more to deliver," Jason replied. "I'm swinging by Tyler's place next."

"You can leave it with me," Jessie said. "He'll be here in an hour. I'll give it to him."

"Netflix and chill for you guys tonight?"

"Watch it," she said.

Jason laughed. "You guys are next."

"Get out of my house, Jason," she said, opening her front door and pointing toward the driveway. "And while I'm at it, this is your official reminder not to do anything stupid this time."

After leaving Emily's best friend's place, Jason swung by the clinic and delivered invitations to Mel and Kathleen—and peeked at the patient records for one final address.

Jason pulled his Jeep into a cul-de-sac of neatly landscaped townhomes, looking for the number he'd scribbled down on a scrap of paper.

Straightening his shirt, he rang the bell.

After a moment, the front door opened to reveal a Pomeranian, voicing his displeasure at Jason's unannounced visit with a single, fierce yap.

"Hello, Tootles," he said, and bent to greet the little dog. "I'm sorry to bother you at home, Mrs. Selby," he said, straightening. "But I wanted to give you this."

THIRTY-TWO

Jason opened his eyes to the bright morning sun and rolled over, stretching. Em was already awake, her eyes luminescent.

Stunning, he thought. *Hard to believe she's mine, and hard to believe this day is finally here.*

"So today is the big surprise," she said. "I'll make sure to dress in my scuba gear and five-inch heels. And pack a lunch and a French horn."

"About that," he began. "I'm hoping you can take Molly and Flint for the morning. I have a few appointments I need to take care of."

Em blinked. "Yeah, sure. Snaggles will be thrilled to have playmates. I'm sure they'll get into a ton of trouble together."

His phone buzzed with the text from Hope, confirming the delivery of the arrangements and Em's bouquet. He scooped up his cell and dashed into the bathroom to respond.

"I...uh...have to get going," he said, glancing at Em one last time from the hallway. "See you later, okay?"

A couple of minutes talking to Cass at Gulf and Main would soothe his nerves.

Certainly.

Absolutely.

Because if they didn't—he didn't want to think about that.

Jason pulled his Jeep into the pub's generous parking lot, empty except for Cass's truck alongside the building. He had roughly an hour to kill—and he knew planting himself on a barstool here would be as good a distraction as any, even if the pub was technically closed.

"Hey, big guy," Cass said as he strode in the door. She gave him a once over. "Wedding day jitters?"

Jason leaned onto the bar and sighed. "Yes? No? I mean, maybe…" He swallowed. Damn. Why was he so jumpy?

Taking a deep breath and letting it out slowly, he pictured Em standing on the beach waiting for him, and his nerves calmed a fraction. "The truth? I'm fucking terrified—and out of my mind excited."

Cass gifted him one of her rare smiles. "It's going to be great."

"I sure as hell hope so."

"A drink to ease those nerves?"

"Not until later," he said. "I'll take a Coke, though."

She filled a glass and set it in front of him. "Listen, I have to get the inventory done before I lock up. Callie's left already—she said something about needing to get her nails done before the wedding. Why don't you hang out here and we'll walk out together? It'll only take me a couple of minutes to finish up."

Cass disappeared and Jason made himself busy by looking through his email on his cell. Sitting at the bar at Gulf and Main, even with the pub empty, was far better than sitting alone at home suffering as minutes slowly ticked by.

The front door swung open. He turned to tell the newcomer that the bar wasn't open until noon. Shock hit him square in the chest.

Mike Fuckface Malone.

"You are not allowed in here," Jason said flatly, standing up, crossing his arms, and gritting his teeth to keep himself from saying anything more.

"Whatever. I'm not here to see you," Mike replied, his eyes sweeping the empty room. "I'm here to see Cass."

Abandoning the rest of his soda, Jason stalked away before he pounded the guy, pushing his way into the backroom in search of Cass. He found her with her pen between her teeth, counting the cases of beer that arrived in the morning shipment.

"Mike Malone is out front," Jason said. "Apparently he needs to talk to you."

"You're shitting me," she said. "That guy's got balls, showing up at my place."

Cass pursed her lips and tossed the clipboard away, wiping her hands on her black apron and tucking her pen inside a pocket. "I'll remind him where the door is," she said.

"You're not welcome in my bar," Cass said to Mike as Jason made his way back to his stool.

"I came to apologize, that's all. And express my regret over what happened," Mike said.

"The person you need to be apologizing to is Emily," Jason spat.

Mike ignored him. "I'm not asking for an invite back here," he said. "I noticed a couple of cars outside and I wanted to stop in and apologize before you opened."

"Okay," Cass said. "You've said your peace. Now show yourself out."

Mike nodded, turning on his heel to go. He caught Jason's eye. There was a strange look on his face—one that could only be described as *triumph*.

"Dick," Jason muttered when the front door fixed in its jamb. "Do you need me to make sure he's gone?"

Cass shook her head. "He might be a dick, but he doesn't strike me as stupid enough to hang around my parking lot." She picked up an empty mixer bottle and started to fill it. "Typical. No promise to change his ways. No remorse—and no accepting responsibility for his actions. But truthfully, that was weird. Why show up here? It's obvious we're closed."

Jason drained his soda and pushed the glass aside. "Don't know, don't care. All I want is to never see that asshole's face again," he said.

"Agreed," Cass said as she bent to count the wine bottles tucked underneath the bar. "Hey, it looks like I have a little more to do than I thought. See you later?"

"See you later," Jason said, standing up.

Cass smiled from across the far end of the bar. "Can't wait."

Damn, Jason was tired.

Exhaustion hit him hard when stepped outside Gulf and Main and into its parking lot. For the briefest of moments, a little voice in his brain said *something's not right*.

He ignored it.

If he'd known he'd be this tired, he would have asked Cass for a Monster instead of a Coke. He sure as hell wasn't going to fall asleep on Em later. He had plans. Big plans. And while those plans included his head on a pillow, they most definitely did *not* include sleeping.

He got behind the wheel, started his car, and let his eyes

drift shut briefly.

Damn, shouldn't have had all that sugar. Who'd have thought?

After pulling out onto Sixteenth Street, he cranked up the radio and switched the air conditioner to the coldest setting. There. That would help until the tiredness abated.

He passed his clinic.

Despite the icy air and the loud music, his eyes slid shut again. He barely managed to jerk them open for a second.

The headlights of an oncoming car suddenly decided they had not one, but two lightbulbs each.

What—

He was aware of his hands slipping off the steering wheel and his head nodding backward.

And the world turned black.

THIRTY-THREE

Jace had only been late once before. And that time, over eight years ago, he'd been so late that he'd never shown up again.

Barefoot, Emily paced her bedroom, tottering between panic and fury as her feet slapped the oak floor. Jace was an hour and a half overdue. His cell was going directly to voicemail, and she'd stopped leaving messages over an hour ago.

After what seemed like the millionth tour of the back of her bedroom, she called Jess.

Her best friend appeared seventeen minutes later, opening the front door while asking, "Any news?" with a solemn Tyler close on her heels.

Emily sunk into the couch and covered her head with her hands. "I can't do this, Jess. It's too much. I can't face every day thinking he's going to disappear again. I can't put myself through it. I won't."

"Hey. Don't make any big decisions right now, okay? Just...let's figure out what happened first," Jess said. "Can your mom tell if he's home?"

"Mom said Jace left about three hours ago in his Jeep. I asked her to call me if he shows up," Emily said. "Do you think he's at the clinic?"

"We drove by the clinic on the way and he's not there," Jess added.

Molly hopped up next to Emily on the couch, snuggling into the crook of her arm.

"Wait. What's Molly doing here?" Jess asked.

"Jace brought her by this morning. He thought Molly and Flint would enjoy hanging here with Snaggles since he was going to be at the clinic with appointments all morning."

Jess and Tyler exchanged a look.

"Where could he be?" Emily said.

Jess sat down next to Emily and took her hand. "I need to ask you something, Em. Did he tell you what plans he had for you two this afternoon?"

Emily blinked and suddenly noticed what Jess and Tyler were wearing: Jess was in a sky-blue summer dress, and Tyler was in a perfectly matching light blue button-down shirt with sleeves rolled up to his elbows, toned, tanned arms showing, and navy pants, tight across his muscled thighs and calves.

Emily shook her head.

"Nothing?"

"No. Just that it was going to be a surprise."

Her best friend and Jace's cousin exchanged another look.

"Are you guys on a date?" Emily asked.

"Us? On a date?" Jess said. "You mean me and Ty? Nah."

"Why would you think that?" Tyler interjected.

"It's just that—"

"Okay," Jess interrupted. "Ty and I are going to drive around town and see if we find his Jeep anywhere. We'll stop by the clinic again. It's possible there was an emergency at the clinic and we missed him on the road."

"But why wouldn't he answer his cell?"

Tyler shifted his weight as if he were uncomfortable with Emily's question.

"I don't know, Em." Jess stood up, straightening her dress. "Stay put. We'll figure this out."

The doorbell rang forty-seven minutes later, jolting Emily out of a reverie.

Finally—

Why is Jace ringing the doorbell? Did he lose his key? Is that why—

She flung open the door, not certain if she was going to hug him or scream at him.

Ryan Billings stood on her front step in the gently falling rain, the blue of his police uniform darkening with every drop.

"Ryan?" she asked, confused. She looked around the beast of a man to see his police cruiser crookedly parked in her driveway, silent blue and red lights blinking on and off.

"Emily," he said in the way of those who are about to impart bad news.

Everything hit her all at once. "What's happened? Where's Jace?"

The glass doors of Westshore Beach Hospital's emergency room slid open with a *woosh*, the cool air conditioning tumbling out to greet Emily as she sprinted inside.

She'd done as much as she could. Gotten shoes on her feet before leaving the townhouse. Made sure Molly, Flint, and Snaggles were inside before locking the door. Clasped her hands together on the ride to stop them from shaking.

Her one concession—Ryan drove.

Thankfully, the innumerable buttons and lights in the dashboard of the police cruiser had been a bit of a distraction along the way. A good distraction. Even so, overwhelming, insidious thoughts had rattled around her brain, some insisting that she run, some demanding that Ryan drive faster.

She'd ignored them all.

Ryan had pulled up to the Westshore Beach Hospital Emergency entrance and she stumbled out of the passenger side, forcing her legs to move toward the sliding glass door.

One step.

Breathe, Emily.

Another step.

One more breath. And another.

Emily paused at the information desk, knees shaking, while Ryan parked the cruiser. "I'm here to see Jason Williams," she said, unable to keep her voice completely steady.

"Your name?" the nurse asked.

"Emily Williams," she recited. *Wait, no, it's not Wil—*

"He's in Triage Room 2B."

I can't go in there, I can't go in there, echoed in Emily's head. *What if Jace—*

"Down the hall, second door on the left," the nurse said, eyes still locked on her computer monitor.

Her feet refused to move. She wanted to speak but no words would come.

The nurse paused her typing and glanced up. "Ms. Williams? Would you like me to show you the way to the room?"

Her hands were clammy; she was sweating. She was going to faint right here, hit her head on the floor, and they would admit her to the hospital.

And she'd die here.

Just like—

She felt the room sway and swallowed thickly.

The triage nurse was out of her chair and around the front of the desk quicker than Emily believed possible. But before the woman reached her, strong hands grasped her from behind and guided her to a chair.

Ryan.

"Slow breaths through your nose, Emily," he said as he crouched in front of her.

Wrong place to sit, she thought. *If I lose my dinner, it's going to be all over your pretty blue uniform and splatter in the general vicinity of, well, everyone in the waiting room. Won't that be fabulous?*

"That's it," Ryan said. "Out your mouth slowly. Good."

She watched him wave off the nurse who was eyeing them both skeptically. *Probably wondering about what my lunch is going to look like all over the linoleum. Honestly, tacos might not be the worst thing that's been splattered on this floor.*

"Thanks," Emily managed after a minute. "Hospitals tend to do that to me."

He nodded. "Would you like me to drive you home? I can speak to the doctor for you and inform Jason you were here."

Emily shook her head. "I think the worst is over. If you don't mind helping me down the hall, I'd like to see him."

Keeping his arm around her, Ryan guided Emily down the hall.

The moment she saw Jace, the panic vanished.

His left eye was swollen shut. His lip was split. His left arm was wrapped in gauze and elevated with some strange metal contraption.

"Hey, you," she whispered, taking his hand gently.

"Em..." His right eye fluttered open. "Em...so sorry." His words were soft and slurred. "I didn't want...I can't ever be...not for you..."

"It's okay, Jace. I'm here," she said gently.

"So much to do...call Hope...Em can't know..."

"Jace," she whispered. "Can you hear me?"

"Secret...Ruby...don't tell Em...ruin everything..."

Her face heated.

What the hell? Who is Hope? And Ruby?

Everything came back in razor-sharp focus: text messages, phone calls.

"...can't find out. Em can't know..." Jace slipped into unconsciousness.

Emily turned to Ryan. "What happened?" she asked.

The police officer removed a small spiral notebook from his shirt pocket and flipped a couple of pages until he found what he was looking for. "At 1:37 p.m., WSPD received a 911 call from a witness, reporting that a car swerved off State Road 31 at Big Bend. Dispatch sent my patrol car to the scene. I found a 2015 Jeep Wrangler off the road on the north side of the bend. The car is registered to Jason Williams. The vehicle had collided with a tree. Mr. Williams was found at the scene, unconscious, and I requested fire and ambulance."

"Oh..."

"I haven't been able to get a statement. However," he continued, "preliminary blood work suggests that the driver, Jason Williams, was exposed to GHB."

"GHB?"

"Gamma-hydroxybutyric acid."

Emily looked at him blankly. "I have no idea what that is," she said.

Ryan tucked his notebook into his breast pocket and

pursed his lips. "It's a date rape drug."

THIRTY-FOUR

Footsteps and the all-too-familiar *thwack* of a metal cart colliding with something—likely a door frame—awoke Jason from a sticky fog of sleep. Groaning, he tried opening his eyes, but his left eye wouldn't budge. His arm throbbed. He was thirsty as hell, and his head hurt like he'd pounded an entire bottle of Jack Daniels the night before.

Light poured in the window, flooding the room and suggesting it was roughly midday. Tyler was folded in a vinyl chair in the corner, hair askew, stubble darkening his jaw, his light blue button-down shirt rumpled as if he'd spent the night in it.

Jason wasn't in the emergency room anymore—he was upstairs in the hospital.

"Where's Em?" Jason croaked, wincing at the pain in his left arm.

"She's over at Jess's place." Squinting, Tyler glanced out the window and into the distance. "She had a hard time with you not showing up."

"Even though I was in here?" Jason gestured around the hospital room helplessly.

"Do you remember what you said to her when you were in the ER last night?"

Jason blinked. "Not really." He looked around for some water. "Why?"

"You said some things that made her uneasy."

"What are you talking about?"

"Perhaps the correct word is *suspicious*," his cousin answered.

Had he spoiled the wedding surprise?

"What the hell happened to me?"

"Looks like you passed out at the wheel. Went off the road at Big Bend. You're one lucky son-of-a-bitch."

"Passed out?" Jason echoed, trying not to nod his head. "Damn. It's so weird. I wasn't tired when I got to Gulf and Main," he said. "But five minutes after I left, I felt like I could nod right off. Came on suddenly. I thought it would pass."

"Yeah. Seems like someone spiked your drink."

"What?" he said. "You've got to be shitting me."

"I'm sure the doctor will be able to give you details. But that's what I was told."

Jason started to look frantically around the room.

"Need something?" Tyler asked.

"My cell," Jason said.

Tyler gestured to Jason's cracked phone on the table on the other side of the bed. "Not operational, I'm afraid."

"My car?"

"Same as your phone, cuz."

"Well, fuck." Jason let his head fall back onto the pillow and closed his eyes as best he could. "I need to talk to Em," he said. "Can I use—"

A nurse strode into the room, wheeling a blood pressure monitor. A doctor followed two steps behind. "Mr. Williams," she said. "Glad to see you awake."

"Not sure I'm glad to be awake," Jason mumbled. "My head is killing me."

The doctor huffed a laugh. "You're lucky to be alive. The accident report says that your car hit a tree."

"Damn," Jason mumbled.

"Exactly," the doctor said with the suggestion of a smile.

"I heard you found something in my blood work?"

"We did. I was in the ER when you were brought in last night. Based on your condition and the circumstances of the accident, I ordered labs."

The nurse bent to wrap his arm in the cuff.

"It seems you ingested a fair amount of a date rape drug by the name of Gamma-hydroxybutyric acid, otherwise known as Liquid Ecstasy."

"Excuse me?"

"Before we continue, I need to inform WSPD that you're awake and able to make a statement," the doctor said, walking toward the door. "I'll be right back."

Tyler leaned closer. "Did you notice anyone suspicious at Gulf and Main before you left? Maybe someone with a bone to pick with you?"

Jason pursed his lips and let out a long breath through his nose. "Actually, I did."

After Ryan drove her home from the emergency room last night, Emily had muted her cell and left the sound off. She had no desire to talk to anyone.

She needed time to think.

Seeing Jace in the emergency room, blood and bruises marring his face, left her numb. It was, strangely— unfortunately—not the entirety of it, though. Somehow, under duress, the man she'd let herself fall in love with again could only talk about shared secrets with other women.

I dodged a bullet, she thought. *I was* this-close *to letting myself trust that man again.*

Taking a deep breath, she pulled on her running shoes and glanced over at her mom, who was sitting at her kitchen table with a coffee.

"I know that look," her mom said.

"And what look is that?"

"You made a decision. A big one. And you don't like it, but you're going to see it through."

"Maybe."

Her mom dug around in her purse and produced an envelope and handed it to Emily. "Before you do what I think you're going to do, make sure you open this." Grabbing her mug, her mom disappeared through the slider onto the deck.

From the other side of the living room, Emily's phone lit up. Tyler again. Abandoning the envelope unopened on her mom's kitchen counter, she crossed the room, turned her cell over, and made her way outside for a run down the beach.

"You need to tell her."

Finally released from the hospital—which felt like drawing a get out of jail free card—Jason bristled at his cousin's words. He glanced over at Tyler at the wheel of his pickup. His cousin was glowering at a tourist driving fifteen miles an hour under the speed limit in front of them.

He'd called Em on Tyler's cell more times than he could remember, explaining to her voice mail that he'd been drugged, and his Jeep and phone were trashed, and he couldn't remember anything that he'd said to her that day in the ER. He'd begged her to come to the hospital. He told her he'd explain everything in more detail when he saw her.

But Em wouldn't answer her cell or call him back, and even though Jason had arranged for a rental car to be delivered tomorrow, he wasn't cleared to drive for another day so he couldn't stop by her townhouse and ask to talk to her in person.

Em should've called. In fact, she should be here right now, driving me home.

"What does it matter?" Jason asked, mounting frustration setting his teeth on edge until he wanted to scream. "If ending up in the emergency room isn't enough of an excuse for being late, then what's the point of our entire relationship? Why would I want to marry someone that won't even give me a chance to explain what happened?"

"You swore everyone to secrecy. Emily needs to know, and since we can't tell her, you have to."

Jason let a long breath and turned to stare out the passenger window.

"Look, I get what you're saying. I do," Tyler said.

"Then what the actual fuck is going on with her?"

"I said she was *suspicious*, remember? She heard you mention other women. She thinks you've been lying. Hiding texts. Keeping secrets from her. She's not wrong, you know."

"What other women? Who?"

"According to Jess—who will undoubtedly swear she did not share the details with me—you mentioned someone by the name of Hope, and someone else by the name of Ruby."

"Hope is the name of the florist and Ruby is the name of the wedding photographer I hired."

Tyler nodded. "Right."

Jason hung his head and raked his fingers through his hair. Not only was his head still sore, everything—absolutely everything—was going to shit.

THIRTY-FIVE

Jace showed up at the foot of her mom's deck, unannounced, as Emily stretched for her morning run.

She'd been successful in avoiding him until this moment.

It had been nearly a week since the accident, and gradually, Jace had stopped texting and calling. He'd stayed inside his house whenever she was at her mom's. She'd stayed inside her mom's place whenever he was on his deck. It was ridiculous, but she could think of no other way to survive.

Emily glanced at him, standing there as if he had something he needed to say. Whatever it turned out to be, it didn't matter. She wasn't wasting a single moment more on Jason The Liar Williams. He could apologize if he wanted to, right now, and then she could get on with her life.

"I came over to tell you that I'm going to go," Jace said without preamble.

Lingering on the sand, he shifted his weight, waiting for her reply. That was no apology. What was he talking about now?

"Go? What does that mean?" she asked, her first words to him since she saw him in the hospital on the day of the accident.

"I'm leaving Westshore Beach. I'm selling the clinic. I'll start over somewhere else."

"Your practice..." she said incredulously. "You worked so hard to build it..."

"I don't care. I should never have moved here. I don't want to hurt you anymore, Em. Never again."

She looked beyond him to the Gulf.

"I didn't want to disappear without saying goodbye. I want you to know that I love you. I always have, and I always will." He glanced to the shoreline she'd been watching a moment ago. "This isn't what I had planned. It's not how I wanted things to play out between us. But, like I said, I don't want to hurt you anymore. I don't want you to live your life every day wondering if you can trust me or if I'm going to vanish again."

Jace nodded, gave her a sad smile, and turned and walked back to his cottage, pulling the door shut behind him without a backward glance.

Emily stood in shock, staring at the door Jace had closed behind him, unable to process what had just happened.

Leaving. That man—that man that had owned her heart— was always leaving her. Always doing the one thing that destroyed her.

Stumbling through her mom's kitchen, she crumpled into the closest chair. She felt hollow and numb, like her heart had been carved out of her chest, and all that remained was a hole far deeper than the one he'd left the day he didn't show up in Mexico.

And this time, she was going to let him walk away.

Let him go without a fight.

But that didn't mean it didn't hurt.

As she drew her legs to her chest, a small white envelope drifted off the counter and floated to the floor, encouraged by a tender gulf breeze flowing in from the open kitchen window.

Before you do what I think you're going to do, make sure you open this.

She'd forgotten all about it.

The envelope was thick and white and heavy, with her mom's name across the front in gorgeous hand-drawn calligraphy. Inside were two smaller, inner envelopes.

She opened the first.

Enclosed was a note addressed to her mom.

Mrs. Lanson,

Would you please save these receipts for me? I don't want to leave them in the cottage for Em to find. I'm not sure that I need to keep them, but just in case—

Thanks!
Jason

A receipt for Danny's Lions, for a bouquet, boutonniere, and four arrangements, signed by Hope Rivera.

A receipt for Westshore Beach Studios, signed by Ruby Shay, photographer.

A receipt for Tikka Masala Restaurant, for catering.

She remembered Jess and Tyler the day of the accident. Her sky-blue dress. The flower on his lapel.

No. Couldn't be.

She pulled the outer envelope open wider, but the second interior envelope, swollen with its contents, refused to budge.

Through the open kitchen window, she heard the chirp of Jace's rental car as it unlocked, and the engine start with *vroom*.

She'd been such a fool.

Emily ran out the front door with the second envelope in hand, the paper inside still unread.

She bolted across the driveway. "Wait," she called. "Jace!"

THIRTY-SIX

Eight weeks later

The day of Emily and Jason's wedding, Westshore Beach, Florida

Emily reminded herself for the thousandth time not to pace. It was a bit difficult anyway with her sandals constantly sinking into the warm, sugary, Florida sand.

I could keep my sandals on and stop pacing. Or I could take my sandals off and keep pacing.

She flicked the offending footwear off and tossed them toward her best friend, standing hand in hand with Jace's cousin. Jess raised an eyebrow and rolled her eyes.

He'll be here. He will.

Snaggles refused to stray from Emily's side, watching as she carved another trough through the sand, this time with her bare feet. Molly was leaping up and down the beach, clearly overdue for a longer run, while the puppies were enjoying the reunion with their siblings, ears flopping as they bounced around the shoreline. Flint was still larger than his littermates, but his puppy belly had thinned to one more appropriate for a gangly adolescent.

To her left, the breeze gently stirred the flowers lining the makeshift aisle—the one she would be walking down in less than an hour—and fluttered the chiffon of her best friend's blue dress.

Emily stopped pacing momentarily to gaze out across the water. Today, the Gulf of Mexico was calm and peaceful, suggesting everything in the world was finally *right*.

Nearly nine years ago, she was supposed to marry the love of her life on a beach, on the Gulf's other side.

Now, of all things, she was waiting for him to return from the airport.

An hour before, Jace left for a last-minute errand—to pick up his brother at the Southwest Florida Regional Airport. Conner's original flight had been delayed by weather somewhere on the west coast, but he'd managed to find a seat on another plane that would get him to Westshore Beach just in time for the ceremony.

Emily had only met Jace's brother once before.

She'd forced herself not to ask for the details of Conner's flight. She'd forced herself not to look in Jace's closet to see if his solitary suitcase was gone. Forced herself not to text him, not to call.

Technically, he doesn't need a suitcase to disappear, she reminded herself. *He's got his cell phone and a car. And he's going to* an airport.

Trust. She would trust him. Trust that he'd come back.

After all, wasn't trust the basis for everything she'd promise him today?

The handful of guests milled around, all smiles, seemingly unconcerned that the groom was nowhere in sight.

From her deck, her mom gave Emily a brief wave and a warm smile, descending the stairs toward the dozen white chairs in two neat rows facing a white gazebo that they'd rented for the ceremony from the florist downtown. Peonies were draped along the rails of Jason's deck—soon to be *their* deck, she supposed—matching the ones decorating the gazebo and completing her bouquet.

An elderly woman dressed from head to toe in peach—including gloves and a hat—sat in the second row of chairs, talking quietly to the small dog on her lap. As she watched, her mom sat down next to the woman and introduced herself.

Emily walked back inside and drifted past the bedroom mirror. Surprisingly, the wedding dress her mom had saved for nearly a decade—unbeknownst to Emily—fit nearly as well as it had when she'd first planned to wear it on the other side of the Gulf.

She glanced at the alarm clock on Jace's side of the bed.

Another minute and he would be late.

The sound of a car, slamming doors, and two male voices drifted in the window from the driveway.

Emily darted to the living room and out the cottage's side door.

She rounded the corner.

And Jace was there.

BONUS SCENE

If you've fallen in love with Jason and Emily's story and would enjoy reading a bonus scene (their wedding!), simply visit:

julietbrandywine.com/the-gulf-between-us-bonus

The Gulf Between Us is a special story to me personally. If you have a moment to share an honest review, please consider going to Amazon or Goodreads and letting me know what you thought of it. It helps more than you know.

I sincerely hope you enjoyed *The Gulf Between Us!* Read on for a sneak peek of Jessie and Tyler's book, *The Further We Fall*, Book Two in The Westshore Beach Series.

Here's to love, second chances, and always, happy endings.

Juliet

The Further We Fall

The Westshore Beach Series, Book Two

Sneak Peek

Ten years ago

Jessie Langston loved to fly.

At least, Jessie amended silently after yet another stomach-dipping drop, she thought she did. When she was a little girl, she dreamed of piloting her own plane, of escaping toward a breathtaking sunset, clouds aglow around her, free to go anywhere. By the time Jessie was in high school, she'd saved enough money to start flying lessons at the tiny airport near her Florida hometown. Even though she exhausted her savings long before she got her license, she always thought she would finish it someday.

And although she hadn't returned to the cockpit since high school, Jessie still loved being in the air.

Until today.

Cutting a jagged north-south path just west of Denver, the Rocky Mountains caused riotous bumps and dips even in mild weather, their stony peaks disturbing the air just enough to make approaches into the airport a bit, well, *interesting*. But as many times as Jessie had flown into Denver on her way back home, the turbulence had never been quite this bad.

Yet *another* nauseating drop had her fumbling with her seat belt to tighten it as far as it could go.

Jessie glanced to her right at the man sitting next to her in the middle seat, engrossed in a book. He seemed not to notice that they were being tossed about like buoys in the middle of a particularly nasty Albuquerque Low.

Apparently, the winter weather was in collusion with the mountain range.

Three dings sounded and the fore flight attendant picked up his mysterious double-secret bat phone and spoke too softly for Jessie to hear. A moment later, the captain's voice came over the 737's intercom.

"Ladies and gentlemen, I'm turning on the fasten seatbelt sign. Please remain in your seats with your seatbelts securely fastened until we're at the gate in Denver."

Fabuloso. Indoor skydiving, anyone?

Jessie risked another quick glance at the guy next to her. He had short dark hair and the wispy beginnings of a beard over a chiseled jaw. His sleeves were rolled up to the elbow, one tan forearm resting on the armrest between them languidly.

She frowned. *You'd think he would have sat in the seat along the aisle and given us both more room.*

The plane settled into a steady, bumpy rhythm like a speedboat slicing through rough water, reminding her that pilots called the condition a *light chop*. She gripped the armrest under the window harder, then forced her fingers to let go and folded her hands in her lap like an actual, fully grown adult.

It's fine. Absolutely fine. Just picture a boat. Row, row, row your—

One moment everything actually *was* fine; the next, a precipitous drop launched her belly into freefall, her stomach plunging.

How far are we falling? How far can we—

With a gasp, she scrambled for the armrest. Except an arm was already there.

The plane leveled out.

The couple in the row behind her chuckled nervously.

"Sorry," she managed, horrified.

The guy next to her glanced up as she removed her grip from his arm, smiled vaguely, then shifted in his seat—angling his long legs toward the aisle and the empty seat next to him.

And started reading again.

"All flights departing Denver International Airport have been canceled. Travelers are advised to contact their individual airlines for assistance."

Jessie was standing in a crowd with the other passengers of Flight 287 staring at a stationary baggage carousel, post-adrenalin fatigue beginning to settle deeply in her bones. Several people groaned at the emotionless announcement that had been repeated every two minutes since they deplaned.

She wondered how long she'd have to wait until flights resumed. At least her luggage would be joining her on the wait.

"Max, one hundred feet."

"I'm sorry?" Jessie said, turning around.

Her row mate was standing behind her.

He shifted his weight. "During turbulence, the maximum a plane moves vertically is about one hundred feet. It feels like much more because of the speed of the plane. Granted, one hundred feet is the height of a ten-story building—"

She blinked. He smiled as she continued to stare.

"Back on the plane, you asked how far we were falling," he said levelly.

"Right." Remembering how she had latched on his arm by accident while they were plunging earthward, she felt her face heat. "I hadn't realized that I'd asked that out loud. Thanks, um, for letting me know."

He continued, "Assuming a conservative cruising altitude, say 32,000 feet, one hundred feet is a drop of around point three percent. Most planes fly higher than that, so the percentage is even smaller."

"You know a lot about aircraft," Jessie said.

He held up his phone. "Nope. Just know how to use Google."

A minute of silence.

"I'm Tyler." He offered his hand for her to shake. "My friends call me Ty."

His grip was strong and came with a devastating smile.

She swallowed. "I'm Jessie."

The baggage carousel chose that moment to beep several warnings that the belt was about to start.

Jessie glanced at his large, black duffel bag, trying to think of some way to continue the conversation. "That's a pretty large carry-on."

"Business trip," he mumbled, scanning the belt.

She nodded, disappointed.

He spotted his bag and yanked it off the carousel, then turned back to her. "Sorry. Didn't mean to ignore you. I have this thing about getting my bag right away."

"Are you on your way home or headed out of town?" she asked.

"On my way back home from Sabi Sands."

Her brow folded in confusion.

"South Africa," he supplied.

"Oh," she said. "Wow."

"Sabi is a perfect place to shoot lion, leopard, elephant, rhino, and buffalo—the Big Five."

She felt her eyes widen. "You mean like actually—"

Tyler chuckled. "I mean take photos of, not actually shoot." He nodded at his carry-on. "That's my camera equipment. I'm a wildlife photographer."

The belt continued its loop around, offering bag after bag to the dwindling crowd. She saw hers and ignored it. "That's incredibly cool," she said.

"What do you do?"

"Nothing nearly as exciting as you do," Jessie said. "I'm a graduate student. I'll be getting my master's degree in education in May."

"You can't tell me that isn't exciting."

"The kids do act like animals at times."

Tyler huffed another laugh.

Her bag passed them forlornly, the straps scraping and thumping against the chrome sides of the carousel.

"Are you going to get your bag one of these times it passes by?" he asked.

Jessie felt her face heat again. "I guess I'm not all that subtle."

"I'm good at observing people," he said, his dark gaze catching on her mouth. "So, what are you doing while we wait for another flight?"

She took a deep breath. Attractive as he was, she didn't

really know him. "I'm not sure," she said after a moment.

"We could grab something to eat, and I can tell you about what it's like to shoot animals," he said, adding a smirk, "and you can tell me what it's like to teach them."

It was her turn to laugh.

Tyler sauntered over to the baggage carousel and retrieved her ancient suitcase.

It wasn't as though she'd be leaving the building with him. Besides, if he happened to be a creep, if she didn't share any personal information, he'd never know how to find her. And he seemed nice enough.

When was the last time she shared a meal with someone outside of class?

It wasn't as if he'd asked her out on bona fide date.

"Ok, then," Jessie said, offering Tyler a tentative smile. "Let's eat."

ACKNOWLEDGEMENTS

To my family who supported me, my friends who encouraged me, and all those who challenged me—thank you. And in case anyone is curious, there's nothing like publishing a book in the middle of packing up and moving two thousand miles across the country.

Special thanks to Douglas County Libraries, Douglas County, Colorado, where the majority of this book was written.

ABOUT THE AUTHOR

Juliet Brandywine is a native Floridian who loves key lime pie, palm trees, and manatees in equal measure. Born already knowing how to read, Juliet is the only person she knows who was endlessly chastened by her parents for having her nose in a book.

She believes in fairytales, love at first sight, and found family, and has a sneaking suspicion that dogs are angels in disguise.

Made in United States
North Haven, CT
25 July 2023

39513258R00168